Oh no

What i

It's the

It can't

tomorr

Ah, but Vernon Bright's been messing about with the laws of gravity.

Can he do that? Last time you broke the law, this policeman came round, and he said …

Our readers don't want to know about that – anyway, it's not that sort of law.

So he doesn't get in trouble then?

Oh yes he does – and so does John, and Dodgy Dave, and Mr Hardman – and when Bright really gets going, the whole planet's in trouble!

So it's definitely the End of the

Could be. You'll have to rea

Steve Barlow is tall and hairy. Steve Skidmore isn't.

They have written quite a few books together. Barlow does the vowels, Skidmore does the consonants. They generally leave the punctuation to sort itself out. They like writing, especially when it gets them out of doing the shopping, the ironing or the washing-up.

Their other Puffin books include the Mad Myths series, which they say is fast, furious, fantastic and frightfully silly.

You can find out more about Steve Barlow and Steve Skidmore on the Web. Visit them at www.puffin.co.uk

Some other books by
Steve Barlow and Steve Skidmore

VERNON BRIGHT AND THE
MAGNETIC BANANA

VERNON BRIGHT AND
FRANKENSTEIN'S HAMSTER

VERNON BRIGHT AND THE
FASTER-THAN-LIGHT SHOW

MAD MYTHS: STONE ME!

MAD MYTHS: MIND THE DOOR!

MAD MYTHS: A TOUCH OF WIND!

MAD MYTHS: MUST FLY!

STEVE BARLOW AND STEVE SKIDMORE

Vernon Bright and

THE END OF THE WORLD

Illustrated by
GEO PARKIN

PUFFIN BOOKS

PUFFIN BOOKS

Published by the Penguin Group
Penguin Books Ltd, 80 Strand, London WC2R 0RL, England
Penguin Putnam Inc., 375 Hudson Street, New York, New York 10014, USA
Penguin Books Australia Ltd, 250 Camberwell Road, Camberwell, Victoria 3124, Australia
Penguin Books Canada Ltd, 10 Alcorn Avenue, Toronto, Ontario, Canada M4V 3B2
Penguin Books India (P) Ltd, 11 Community Centre, Panchsheel Park, New Delhi – 110 017, India
Penguin Books (NZ) Ltd, Cnr Rosedale and Airborne Roads, Albany, Auckland, New Zealand
Penguin Books (South Africa) (Pty) Ltd, 24 Sturdee Avenue, Rosebank 2196, South Africa

Penguin Books Ltd, Registered Offices: 80 Strand, London WC2R 0RL, England

www.penguin.com

First published 2002

2

Text copyright © Steve Barlow and Steve Skidmore, 2002
Illustrations copyright © Geo Parkin, 2002
All rights reserved

The moral right of the authors and illustrator has been asserted

Set in Palatino

Made and printed in England by Clays Ltd, St Ives plc

British Library Cataloguing in Publication Data
A CIP catalogue record for this book is available from the British Library

ISBN 0–141–30587–8

CONTENTS

The authors would like to thank Trevor Day for his invaluable advice on the scientific principles referred to in this book, and for pointing out which of our ideas were 'come on, boys, that's totally impossible' and which were merely 'completely gaga, but what the heck, it's sci-fi'. Any remaining inaccuracies are what we managed to slip in while he was looking the other way.

Please note:
Readers should not attempt to generate previously undiscovered fundamental particles in their own home. This may result in the destruction of the world, and is therefore a job for scientists.

Antigravitons can contribute to weight loss only as part of a calorie-controlled diet.

CHAPTER ONE

Mr Hardman's Trying Circuits

'You are a bunch of namby-pamby mummy's boys!' bawled Mr Hardman, teacher of PE, Elmley School. 'What are you?'

Class 8F, Elmley School wheezed breathlessly as one. 'We – uh – are – uh – b-uh-nch of namby – uh – pamby – uh – m – uh – mummy's boys.'

'That's right!' snarled Mr Hardman, staring icily as his trembling victims gulped air like freshly caught fish and rubbed at their aching muscles.

John Watt shook his head and tried to suck oxygen into his protesting lungs. He hated this type of PE lesson. Even his friend Vernon Bright, who was brilliant at most sports (and science and

1

maths and practically everything else, as he kept reminding anyone who would listen) heartily disliked the hour in the gym with Mr Hardman.

'If you're going to have any chance in the staff-versus-students basketball match, then you need to be fit!' screamed the PE teacher. 'Otherwise, we'll thrash you.' He gave a wolfish grin. 'Like we always do,' he added smugly.

John wasn't looking forward to the annual staff-versus-boys basketball match. The staff always won, mainly because Mr Hardman always picked the student team. This year, he'd picked John.

'But I'm useless at basketball,' John had protested.

'Of course you are,' Bright had said. 'He only picks useless players. Why d'you think the staff always win?'

To make absolutely sure that the staff's one-hundred-per-cent winning record was never challenged, Mr Hardman also spent the weeks leading up to the match forcing the boys to do circuit training. He set them a series of muscle-straining, tendon-stretching and bone-crunching physical exercises designed to reduce them to knock-kneed, broken-winded, gibbering physical wrecks. As an ex-Marine (rumoured to have been thrown out of the armed services for excessive cruelty) Mr Hardman lived by the rule that any form of exercise that didn't leave his pupils screaming in agony, gasping for breath or being physically sick was not worth doing.

'The object of the exercise,' barked Mr Hardman, 'is to build up your pathetic and miserable characters, as well as your feeble bodies. In the Marines,' he went on, 'this is called circuit training.'

'In the real world, it's called torture,' moaned his students.

These tortures included push-ups, pull-ups, sit-ups, press-ups and chin-ups: all of which gave the class a near-fatal dose of the fed-ups. Squat thrusts, rope climbing, weightlifting and star jumps completed the energy-sapping and body-destroying circuit.

At the sound of Mr Hardman's whistle, all the boys had to begin one hundred and twenty seconds of physical agony. At the end of this time, Mr Hardman blew his whistle again and the class had to run to the next exercise to endure another couple of minutes of hell.

At the moment, the class were being allowed a

brief respite as Mr Hardman berated them for being useless. 'Call yourselves men?' screamed the teacher. 'You are a bunch of big girls' blouses.'

'That's sexist,' panted John to Bright.

'He *is* sexist,' Terry McBride butted in. 'That's why he won't let any girls play in the basketball team.'

'Well, somebody should tell him,' said John.

'Why don't *you* tell him?' murmured Bright, under what breath he had left.

John looked up at the triangular-chested PE teacher. Mr Hardman's short, cropped ginger hair accentuated his bullet-shaped head. He was red-faced from continual bawling, and the veins stood out in his neck, pulsing violently as blood beat its angry way around the muscled body. John decided, on balance, that informing Mr Hardman he was being sexist was not a particularly clever idea. Not if John wanted to keep all his body parts intact and in the right places.

'Big girls' blouses!' repeated Mr Hardman for good measure. 'What are you?'

'We are a bunch of big girls' blouses,' chanted the class, John included. Bright remained tight-lipped. 'Chicken,' he hissed at John.

'Realist,' John hissed back. 'You wouldn't dare say anything to Hardman.'

Bright glared at John. If there was one thing Bright couldn't resist, it was a challenge. Tell Bright that he couldn't do something and he'd do his level best to prove you wrong by doing it. Unfortunately, Bright never thought about the consequences of his actions. If he was told that he couldn't destroy the world, he'd do his utmost to prove that he could, regardless of the resulting catastrophe.

Luckily, before Bright could respond to John's challenge, Mr Hardman blew his whistle. 'Next exercise! Move!' The class were startled into action. They leaped across the gym, clattering and sliding into each other in their anxiety to be at their appointed exercise station before Hardman blew his whistle again.

'Hurryupatthedoublemoveitmoveit, MOVE IT!'

Bright, John and Terry hurried to their assigned area and waited for the next whistle. A couple more wheezing victims joined them to make up their small group.

'Two minutes; begin!' *PEEP!* Hardman's whistle echoed across the gym.

The class lurched into frenzied action. Bright's group alternately reached for the ceiling and bent double as Mr Hardman prowled round the gym, yelling out encouragement and insults. Mainly the latter.

'If we were meant to touch our toes, they'd have been placed further up our bodies,' moaned John as his spine creaked.

Bright humphed. 'Nonsense! Our bodies are perfectly designed to meet our needs. They're the result of hundreds of thousands of years of evolution.' He glanced up at Hardman. 'Mind you, some people are still at the Neanderthal stage.'

'Bright,' wheezed Terry, 'how do you know when you're having a heart attack?'

'You get a pain in the arm ...'

'I've got that.'

'Followed by a tightening of the chest,' continued Bright.

'I've got that as well! Quick, call for the trauma team!'

'I'll call you an undertaker and cut out the middle man!' bawled Mr Hardman as he stood over the 'dying' casualty. 'Stop moaning and put some effort into it, McBride. I've already had enough of you this lesson!'

Terry was in Mr Hardman's bad books for committing the greatest sin in the PE world. The unforgivable misdeed. The unpardonable crime.

He had forgotten his PE kit.

Mr Hardman had said nothing but headed into the changing room, emerging a few seconds later with a cardboard box.

The blood drained from Terry's face. 'Oh no, sir, not the lost property box!'

'Oh yes, McBride, the lost property box. Get 'em on!' Hardman threw Terry a pair of mould-covered shorts followed by a pink top with little flowers on the front (originally found in the girls' changing room).

'Oh no, sir! You must be kidding!'

'Do I look as if I'm kidding, McBride? Put 'em on.'

The rest of the class guffawed in an unsupportive way. Even Bright, who wasn't known for his sense of humour, sniggered.

'But I haven't got any trainers ...' Terry protested weakly.

'Oh, don't worry.' Grinning like the cold-blooded reptile that he was, Mr Hardman threw a pair of black plimsolls at Terry's head. 'One size fits all,' he barked.

Terry inspected the offending pumps. 'They're size eleven,' he protested. 'I'm size six.'

'You can get your feet in them, can't you?' snapped Mr Hardman.

'Yeah, but ...'

'Then they fit! One size fits all!'

The unfortunate Terry had spent the lesson flopping from one exercise to the next with Mr Hardman continually on his back. 'Who do you think you are, McBride? Mr Floppy, the happy, clappy clown? Get a move on!'

Now, standing over the semi-comatose Terry, Mr Hardman blew his whistle. 'Only another five minutes of this, then you can have a nice cold shower. Get ready for the next exercise!'

'Oh, great!' moaned John. 'Sit-ups.'

John, Bright, Terry and the other luckless members of their group arranged themselves on their backs, side by side with their feet jammed under the bottom wall bar. They clasped their hands behind their heads. At the sound of Mr Hardman's whistle, they began heaving their protesting torsos into a sitting position: up, down … up, down …

'This is inhuman!' Terry was still moaning. 'There ought to be a law.'

'There is.' Bright was unsympathetic. 'The more weight you carry, the more effort it takes to move it. If you didn't eat so many chips, you wouldn't weigh as much and you wouldn't find it so hard to drag yourself off the ground. There's no appeal against the law of gravity.'

'Never mind, Tel,' croaked Mick Philips. 'A few more days of this and you'll have a six-pack.'

'If I want a six-pack, I can go to Tesco …'

'Hey, Terry!' Simon West wheezed between gulping breaths. 'I think I recognize those shorts. Didn't they belong to Smoky Robinson?'

''What, the singer?' rasped Mick. 'My mum likes him.'

'No, you div. Keith Robinson. The bloke in Year Eleven.'

'Why do they call him Smoky?'

'Always round the back of the groundsman's hut, isn't he? By the way, Terry, should you be rattling like that?'

'What? Who's rattling?'

'You are. When you sit up. Well, it's more a scratching noise, really.'

Terry frowned. 'Must be something in the pockets ...'

At that moment, there was a sudden, loud fizzing noise and the front of Terry's shorts caught fire.

'Yeah, they're Smoky's,' said Mick. 'He always carries matches in his ...'

'Aaaargh!' Terry leaped up and danced around, slapping furiously at himself. The exercises stopped. As they saw what was happening, some of Terry's classmates found their eyes watering in sympathy. Others instinctively clasped their hands in the 'free-kick defensive-wall' position. A horrified sigh ran round the gym. 'Ooooooh!'

The air was filled with the odour of wet bonfires as the dreadful shorts smouldered. With a final anguished howl, Terry hauled them off and flung them away. He hopped around the gym in his underpants, trying at the same time to blow on the affected bits. Seconds later he gave up and collapsed on the floor in agony. 'Hot!' he shrieked. 'Hot! Hot! Hot!'

'Hang on, McBride!' Mr Hardman grabbed a fire extinguisher. He directed the nozzle at the smoking Terry and

squeezed the trigger. White vapour sprayed from the funnel and bathed Terry's midsection.

'Excuse me, sir.'

'Not now, Bright!' snapped Mr Hardman. 'I'm trying to stop McBride going up in smoke, in case you hadn't noticed!'

'Yes, sir. But that's a CO_2 fire extinguisher. I don't think you're supposed to use it on people.'

Mr Hardman stopped spraying. 'Why not?'

'Because it produces carbon dioxide gas at very low temperatures. If you spray him for long enough, you'll fast-
freeze his ...'

'All right, Bright! Point taken.'

Terry had by now dragged his shivering body into a foetal crouch. 'Cold!' he hissed through chattering teeth. 'Cold! Cold! Cold!'

'Give him air!' ordered Mr Hardman. The class obeyed and moved back.

Mr Hardman stood over the twitching Terry. 'Are you in pain, McBride?'

'Yes, sir,' whimpered Terry, thankful for some sympathy.

'Serves you right for carrying matches!' snapped Mr Hardman. 'Let that be a lesson to you! No pain, no gain.'

'No pain, no brain,' whispered Bright to John.

Mr Hardman shot round. 'Did someone say something?' he demanded.

The class remained silent as Mr Hardman pushed his face forward. 'Someone said something. Who was it?'

John stared at Bright. 'Chicken,' he hissed.

Bright's eyes flashed. His hand shot up. 'It was me, sir. I said "No pain, no brain", sir.'

'And what do you mean by that?'

Bright smiled. 'Just what I said, sir. It's a scientific fact. Pain is a warning signal. It's a message sent to the brain by receptors, nerves and neurons. If you can't feel pain, sir, then your brain isn't working properly. I'm sure you can feel pain though, sir.' Bright paused momentarily. 'Can't you?'

John winced. Was Bright being deliberately rude, or just being his usual arrogant self? It was difficult to tell.

Mr Hardman was obviously having the same thought. He and Bright had experienced several run-ins. Run-ins that had usually seen Bright winning the gold medal and leaving the teacher licking his wounds. Sometimes literally.

'You think you're clever, don't you, Bright?'

Bright raised his eyebrows. 'Actually, yes, sir. I recently took an IQ test and scored over 165. That's above the genius scale.'

The unfortunate Terry had been forgotten as the class listened intently to the confrontation between teacher and pupil.

'All right, Bright. You think you're bright, don't you, Bright! You think you're always right, Bright. Bright's a bright spark. A real bright lad!'

John grimaced and felt sorry for Bright. Bright loathed people making fun of his name. And although most people did, John didn't expect teachers to do so. Then again, Mr Hardman wasn't the usual sort of teacher.

'You might be brainy, Bright, but that doesn't matter. Not in the real world. Out there it's survival of the fittest.'

'You're talking about Darwin now?' asked Bright.

'No, lad, I'm talking about muscles!' snapped Mr Hardman. 'Muscles and strength. Things that you haven't got.' He stared at Bright's arms and sneered. 'I have seen more muscles on a sparrow's kneecap.'

'You can't directly compare the two,' replied Bright. 'Sparrows' knees bend backwards, whereas human knees bend in the opposite ...'

'I don't care!' The PE teacher was seriously close to losing it completely. 'You need taking down a peg or ten!' he snarled.

'I think you'll find that brains will always beat brawn,' said Bright.

'You think so?' Mr Hardman's cheek twitched. 'Right, Bright! A challenge. Your brains (Hah!) against my muscles.'

'A challenge!' Bright nodded. 'All right. Anything you say.'

'Right!' Mr Hardman gave a cry of triumph. 'You heard that, lads. Anything I say.' He pointed to a set of weights. 'How about a weightlifting challenge, Bright?' He stuck his face towards

Bright's, nose to nose. 'See who can lift the heaviest weight. Or is that a bit too much for you?'

A silence fell on the gym.

John gulped. It was ridiculous. Bright versus Hardman at weightlifting? Surely Bright would see sense and back down …

'I accept!'

There was a buzz of excitement.

A look of maniacal joy spread itself across Hardman's face. The class stood with mouths open and tongues hanging out.

'Right, come on.' Mr Hardman headed towards the weights.

DRRRRIIIIINNNNGGGGG!

The school bell pierced the tension.

'Saved by the bell!' cried John. 'We can't be late for next lesson.'

Mr Hardman looked daggers at him before shaking his head. He stared hard at Bright. 'All right. Next week's lesson. Same time, same place, same challenge. You have one week, Bright.'

Bright stood defiant.

Mr Hardman laughed maliciously. 'Then we'll see what can lift more weight – your brain, or my muscles!'

'Well, this time you've really gone and done it.' John shook his head mournfully. 'You and your big mouth.'

Bright merely shrugged in reply.

School was over and the two boys were trudging through the back streets on their way to Dodgy Dave's. Bright had to pick up some supplies that he needed for one of his experiments.

'There's no way you can get out of it,' continued John. 'Everyone wants to know what's going to happen.'

This was true. The Elmley School rumour service had nearly achieved meltdown after the PE lesson; all the students knew about Hardman's challenge within minutes. Even some of the teachers had found out and had decided that it would be a good thing for Bright to be taught a lesson, especially as he usually claimed that teachers couldn't teach him anything.

'There's no way you're going to win this one,' stated John. 'Hardman will thrash you out of sight. He's got more muscles than a seafood restaurant.'

'Brain will always beat brawn,' Bright snapped back. 'Science will always find a way.'

John shook his head in exasperation. 'Here we go again. Science, science, science. You reckon *everything* is to do with science.'

'Because it is!' exclaimed Bright. 'Every minute of every day – whether you're eating, sitting, walking, shopping, going to the toilet or fast asleep – it's all science,' he added.

John decided that he had had enough of Bright's superior airs and graces. 'All right then. How does science come into Hardman's gym lessons?'

'Hah!' sneered Bright. 'Where do I begin? The fitness training that Hardman puts us through is all about biology and chemistry. Terry's accident happened because of physics ...'

'I thought it happened because he was wearing Smoky Robinson's shorts.' John winced as he remembered the look on Terry's face and the smell of smouldering cloth. Luckily for Terry, the school nurse had said that his burns would heal up in a couple of days, although there was no hope for the burnt shorts.

Bright ignored him, as usual. 'It happened,' he went on, 'because of physical forces. Firstly, Hardman made us do sit-ups, using the energy in our muscles to overcome the force of gravity. This movement caused friction. The matches in Terry's pocket rubbed against each other, leading to agitation of the molecules ...'

John nodded wisely. 'Yes, I could see his molecules were agitated.'

'... thereby causing spontaneous combustion and releasing heat energy. So, you see,' Bright continued smugly, 'it's all science.'

John was not in the mood to let Bright off the hook. 'OK, here's some science for you,' he said. 'Hardman's muscles are bigger than yours. He is stronger than you. He can lift heavier weights than you. He will beat you!' John held out his palms. '*It's all science*,' he said pointedly.

If John thought that he had got the better of Bright, he was sadly mistaken.

'Ahh! But size doesn't always matter.' Bright smiled. 'Just think about ants.'

John shook his head at this sudden jump of logic. 'Why should I think about ants?'

'Certain species of ants can pick up to fifty times their own body weight. That's more than humans can. It's all to do with spare muscle capacity.'

'So all you've got to do to beat Hardman is grow four more legs and a couple of antennae?' replied John caustically. He looked at Bright's scrawny figure. 'And to be honest, there's not much spare muscle capacity on you.'

Bright glared at John. 'What I'm saying is that this is all relative. Logically, Hardman should beat me. But in relative terms, he won't.'

John's head was spinning with Bright's slipperiness. 'So how, *relatively*, is your brain going to beat Hardman's brawn?' he demanded.

Bright's lips pursed and his shoulders slumped. 'I haven't figured that out yet.'

Bright and John arrived at Dodgy Dave's. Dodgy's real name was David Thomas Vickers, but he was known as Dodgy Dave to everyone else (including the police). And he hadn't got the name because he was good at avoiding bumping into people. He was a supplier of ex-military goods, although this was a term that didn't stand up well to close examination. There was not a lot of 'ex' about many of the goods Dave sold. This suited Bright to a T and he used Dave to supply various pieces of hardware for his experiments. Generally, Bright didn't ask where Dave got his goods from and Dave didn't volunteer the information. It was an arrangement that worked well.

The two boys stepped through a freshly painted gateway into Dave's yard and entered the strange world of military vehicles, ammo boxes and camouflage nets of various colours and sizes.

Dave was at the far end of the yard, carefully inspecting some boxes marked TOP SECRET. He was wearing his usual dark sunglasses, combat suit and black beret. It was a strange outfit to wear in the middle of an English town in the twenty-first century, but Dave *was* strange.

John called out a cheery 'Hello!'

Dave jumped like a startled rabbit and quickly threw a tarpaulin over the boxes. He turned round, his face a deep shade of red with embarrassment and guilt.

'Whoa, boys. Slinky commando-style creep-up.'

Bright gave him a narrow-eyed look. 'What's that you've got under the tarpaulin?'

Dave looked uncomfortable. 'Nothin'! Nothin' under here but some old … er … stuff.'

'Really?' drawled Bright.

Dave spread his arms. 'OK, OK, so maybe it's ultra-top-secret stuff. If I was to tell you about it, I'd have to kill you afterwards.'

Bright rubbed his chin thoughtfully. 'Ultra-top-secret, you say?'

Dave gave a sheepish grin. 'Just forget the whole thing, OK?'

Behind him, the tarpaulin covering the boxes slowly began to rise into the air. Dave jumped, spun round and threw his weight on to the moving mass. It settled down, slowly. Dave half leaned, half lay across the tarpaulin in a totally unconvincing display of nonchalance.

'Have you got an animal under there?' demanded John.

'Hah! Gee! An animal? What are you, nuts? What a crazy idea!' Dave reached over and batted

another moving lump under the tarpaulin. 'Just some hydraulic gizmos, nothin' to interest you boys. Honest Injun.' He turned and swiped frantically as more lumps appeared.

Bright shrugged and whispered to John, 'Leave it. We'll find out soon enough. You know Dave can't keep secrets for long.' He looked around admiringly and raised his voice. 'Nice place you've got now.'

Dave gave a large grin. He looked as pleased as a dog

with a new bone. To be absolutely precise, he looked as pleased as a supplier of ex- (and not so ex-) military goods, whose warehouse was destroyed by an explosion (partly caused by Bright), but whose insurance company had paid up (incredibly), thus allowing him to pay off all his debts (which were considerable) and rebuild a new, bigger and better warehouse.

'That explosion was a godsend,' crowed Dave, securing the straining tarpaulin. 'It helped me get rid of a load of old junk.'

John looked around at the piles of military hardware cluttering up every spare corner of the

yard. Which you've replaced with a load of new junk, he thought.

Dave ushered Bright and John away from the twitching tarpaulin and led them into the new building. 'Crack your jaw, Vernie. Tell me what's happening.'

Bright explained his predicament to Dave. It took some time. Eventually he got to the point. 'So I wondered if you knew anything about weightlifting?'

Dave gave a deep chuckle. 'Do I know anything about weightlifting? Do bears work out in the woods? Did I ever tell you about the time I just missed out on the weightlifting gold medal at the Olympic Games?'

'Which one?'

'Nineteen-forty,' shot back Dave. 'I remember it like it was lunchtime.'

John looked heavenwards. He knew that there hadn't been an Olympic Games in 1940, due to a certain World War II (which Dave also claimed he'd been involved in). As usual, Dave was 'slightly-bending-the-truth' to the point of breaking it.

Bright, however, knew very little about the

history of the Olympic Games. Seeing a glimmer of hope, he began to question Dave. 'So what happened? Did you come second?'

'Er, ahem, er …' Dave spluttered. 'I just missed out on the silver as well …'

There was a pause.

'… and the bronze …'

'So what proof have you got that you were actually there?' asked John pointedly.

Dave looked genuinely hurt. 'No actual physical show-you-in-the-face proof. Just ma word as an honest citizen.'

'Right,' said John.

'So you can help me?' asked Bright.

The 'honest citizen' stared at Bright's physique. A grimace flitted across his face. 'Of course, amigo!' he cried, bending the truth so much it snapped in half. 'You'll have to put the time in. Work out. Pump iron. Eat big. But you could do it.'

Bright's face lit up. 'You think so?'

'One-hundred-per-cent certain! How long we got?'

'A week.'

'No chance.'

Bright's jaw dropped. John sniggered.

'To be honest, Vernie, don't take this personally, but a little skinny runt like you? In a week? You ain't got a prayer.'

Bright looked pained, but took the judgement on the chin. 'Never mind, I'll think of something.' He stared around at the packed shelves and boxes that littered the floor. 'Have those brand-new, nearly surplus, virtual-reality USAF pilot-training helmets come in yet?'

Dave shook his head. 'Ixnay on that one, dude. I'll let you know.'

'Oh, well.' Bright turned to John. 'Are you coming over to the lab?'

John shook his head. 'I've got to get home. Mum's volunteered me to do some babysitting tonight.'

Bright nodded. 'I might pop round later.' He turned to Dave. 'Now, about these new high-powered lasers ...'

'Anuvver one, anuvver one!' Lulu bounced up and down on the sofa. 'Dolly wants anuvver one!'

John groaned. 'I've read Dolly dozens of nursery rhymes already. She can't want more!'

Lulu held the doll up and waggled its plastic

head. 'If Dolly doesn't get anuvver nursewy rhyme, she'll get upset, and if she gets upset, I'll start to cwy …'

'All right, all right!'

John was babysitting for his neighbour. He was looking after Lulu (and her dolly). Lulu was one-hundred-per-cent blonde curls and attitude. Since John's mum and dad had split up, money was tight, so John occasionally did his bit by doing odd jobs. One of these was babysitting. He hated it.

'Anyway, Dolly won't go to sleep unless you read anuvver one!'

John thought of telling Lulu that if he had any more grief from Dolly, he'd shove Dolly's head in the blender, but he decided that this wouldn't help the situation. However, before he could begin another nursery rhyme, there was a knock on the door followed by a shout. 'Hello!'

It was Bright. He stuck his head round the door. 'Haven't you finished yet?'

'Nearly,' sighed John. 'Dolly's being a bit of a pain.'

Bright stared at him. 'What?'

'It doesn't matter. Just sit down, I shouldn't be long.' John picked up the book of nursery rhymes and began to read. *'Hey diddle diddle, the cat and the fiddle, the cow jumped over the moon.'*

'Rubbish!' snorted Bright.

John broke off. 'What is?'

'That is! A cow cannot jump over the moon. It's scientifically impossible.'

Lulu stared blankly at Bright, who began waving his arms around.

'For a start, to overcome the effects of gravity, and actually get into space, the cow would have to achieve escape velocity. It would have to reach a

speed of over eleven kilometres a second, and cows aren't known for their speed.'

'Yes, but ...' John tried in vain to interrupt Bright.

'And then there's the question of how the cow would survive in space. Unless it was wearing a spacesuit – and I don't think you mentioned that – then it would suffocate, freeze and be bombarded with cosmic radiation – which would probably make it grow three extra legs and glow in the dark.'

Lulu hadn't a clue what Bright was going on about, but whatever it was, it didn't sound very nice. Her bottom lip began to quiver.

Bright, though, was unstoppable. 'The lack of pressure in space means the cow's eardrums would burst.' He flung his arms out. 'BANG!'

Lulu jumped off the sofa in shock. Dolly shot into the air.

'And how would a cow travel round the moon and get back to earth?'

Before John could say 'haven't got the foggiest,' Bright answered for him. 'Maybe the moon's gravity could help to push it round, but the cow would need its own power supply. And the

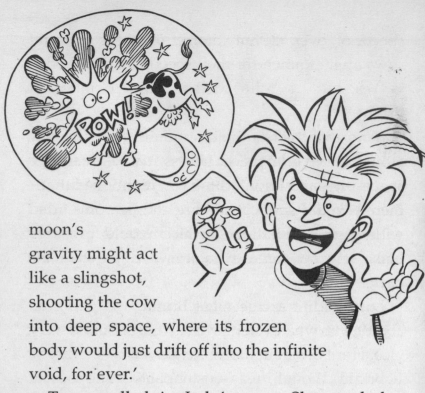

moon's
gravity might act
like a slingshot,
shooting the cow
into deep space, where its frozen
body would just drift off into the infinite
void, for ever.'

Tears welled in Lulu's eyes. She stuck her fingers in Dolly's ears.

'So,' Bright wagged his finger, 'it's all rubbish. Because even if this super cow survived all that, it would simply burn up on re-entry into earth's atmosphere. And it wouldn't be a slightly burnt Sunday roast beef joint! There'd be nothing left at all. The cow would disintegrate!'

'Poor moo-cow!' Lulu pointed accusingly at Bright. 'You made Dolly cwy!' Her face crumpled.

'WHAAAAAAH!' Lulu's wails filled the room.

At that moment John's mum walked through the door.

Thirty minutes later, John and Bright were still sitting in the lounge. There was no Lulu, and no Dolly. John's mum had given John a furious telling-off for upsetting Lulu. Then she had taken the shrieking child and her doll to the local burger bar in an effort to cheer her up with a Jolly Meal (a cheeseburger, small fries and a fizzy drink with enough additives to choke a horse).

'Why do you do things like that?' asked John.

'Because you shouldn't tell lies to kids! I mean, how could a dish run away with a spoon?
Where's the sense?'

'It's just a nursery rhyme! It's not supposed to make sense. Didn't your mum ever tell you any nursery rhymes?'

Bright looked puzzled. 'What for?'

'What for? For fun!'

'No, why should she?' Bright was clearly astonished by the suggestion. 'They're all illogical, ridiculous lies! They're not factually based. They're unscientific.'

John began to realize why Bright was so different from other people. 'They're not supposed to be science. They're entertainment. When you hear about a cow jumping over the moon, you automatically say "that's impossible because of the effect of gravity", but that's not the …'

'Eureka! That's it!' John was cut off mid-sentence by Bright's cry.

'What's it?'

Bright's eyes glittered. 'The effect of gravity. That's how I'm going to beat Hardman!'

CHAPTER THREE

Weight and Gee

'Very nice,' said John dubiously. 'Who is it?'

The following day, after school, Bright and John were standing on the balcony of the top floor of the local museum. Bright was gazing admiringly at a marble head, which stared stonily at them from its plinth.

'Galileo Galilei.'

'Is that his name, or are you trying to yodel?'

Bright ignored the question. 'He's a famous Italian scientist. That's his bust.'

John eyed the small marble statue in disbelief. 'No, it's not. It's his head and shoulders. Men don't have busts.'

'Did your mother drop you on your head when you were small, or what?' Bright pointed at the stone figure. 'A bust is a head-and-shoulders carving of somebody famous. This is Galileo's. What do you think?'

'He's got a big hooter.' John gave the sculpture a critical look. 'You dragged me halfway across town to see this?' he demanded bitterly.

Bright was unrepentant. 'I'm going to explain how I'm going to beat Hardman in a weightlifting contest,' he said. 'I'll start at the beginning and keep it simple.'

John snapped his fingers. 'Oh, I get it! On the morning of the contest, you're going to bash Hardman over the head with this statue and he won't be able to lift any weights because he'll be unconscious.'

Bright sighed. 'I didn't think I'd have to make it *this* simple. Galileo was an astronomer ...'

'You mean he wrote the *"You and Your Stars"* column for the local paper?'

'That's an astrologer. Galileo designed one of the first telescopes in 1609 and discovered the moons of Jupiter.' Bright took off his schoolbag and started to rummage about in it. 'But he was also one of the first scientists to do experiments with gravity.' He pulled a very scuffed cricket ball out of the bag and handed it to John while he rummaged again. 'I'm going to show you one of Galileo's most famous experiments.' Bright straightened up, holding a pencil eraser. 'I want you to imagine that we are standing on the Leaning Tower of Pisa.'

'Pizza? This Galileo made a tower of pizza?' John whistled appreciatively. 'It must have taken him ages. Why didn't he use bricks? Or breeze blocks? I mean, pizza's very thin.'

Bright groaned. 'Listen ...'

'Anyway, why didn't it fall over? I suppose if he made it while the pizza was still hot, all the cheesy bits might stick it together like cement, but what happened when it rained?'

'Pisa!' howled Bright, causing several scholarly-looking men and women to turn and gaze at him with disapproval. 'Pisa!' he hissed more quietly. 'Not pizza! It's a city in Italy.'

A vague recollection of flicking through a travel brochure popped into John's mind. 'Oh, yes. What about it?'

Bright threw the cricket ball up into the air and

caught it. 'Galileo dropped things off it.'

John looked shocked. 'That was a bit dangerous, wasn't it? He might have hurt someone.'

Bright gritted his teeth. He held up the cricket ball and the eraser. 'Which of these is heavier?'

John pointed at the cricket ball.

'So, if I dropped both of these off the balcony, which would land first?'

John shrugged. 'The ball, I suppose.'

Bright smirked. 'Let's see. You go downstairs and get ready to catch.'

A minute later, John stood on the ground floor, peering at Bright, who was leaning over the balcony some twelve metres above him.

Bright's voice floated down. 'Ready?'

John gave him the thumbs-up signal.

Bright thrust his arms out and opened his hands simultaneously.

The cricket ball and the eraser dropped together. They smacked into John's outstretched hands at exactly the same moment. Then, their paths diverged. The cricket ball spun away and bounced off a civil war helmet, while the rubber ricocheted the other way and struck the museum curator a stinging whack on the ear.

Some time later, when they had outdistanced the infuriated curator, Bright said, 'Butterfingers.'

'Well, why d'you think Hardman picked me for the school basketball team?' asked John mournfully. 'Anyway, what was that supposed to prove?'

Bright turned into his street. 'That gravity affects everything. All objects fall at the same rate, no matter how heavy or light they are.'

'Aha!' John pointed a delighted finger at Bright. 'W-R-O-N-G spells wrong! Heavy things fall faster, and I can prove it.'

Bright's glance was a mixture of amusement and contempt. 'Oh, really.'

'Yes, really.' John did a fair impersonation of Bright's voice at its most pompous. 'For the purposes of my experiment, I shall require a marble and a feather.'

'Come down to the lab,' Bright told him. 'I'll see what I can do.'

Bright's laboratory looked much as usual. Tottering piles of equipment occupied most of the floor space that wasn't covered with mounds of books, paper and scientific magazines. Bright sat on a lab stool with his arms folded. John stood on top of the lab bench.

'Observe,' he said importantly. 'In one hand, I

hold a marble, in the other, a feather. I shall drop them at exactly the same time.'

He did so. Almost immediately, the marble clattered on to the floor. The feather swooped down in a series of lazy spirals, and came to rest several seconds later.

John bowed theatrically. 'I rest my case.'

'I should rest your brain if I were you.' Bright picked up the marble and the feather, and dropped them into a long clear tube. He rammed a rubber bung into the open end of the tube. Then he connected one end of a rubber hose to the side of the tube, and the other end to a machine. He switched it on.

'This is a vacuum pump,' he told John. 'It's pumping all the air out of the tube.'

The note of the pump changed. Bright put a clip around the hose, pinching it tight, and switched the machine off.

'Now, there's no air in the tube.' Bright held it up. 'Watch.'

He turned the tube over.

The marble and the feather dropped like stones, and hit the stoppered end of the tube simultaneously.

John stared. 'Do that again.'

Bright did.

John shook his head in wonderment.

'What I should have said earlier,' Bright explained, 'is that all objects fall at the same rate if you ignore the effects of air resistance. A falling object has to push air aside as it falls. This is easier for a small, heavy object like a marble than it is for a comparatively large, light object like a feather. That's why birds fly and elephants don't.'

'Dumbo did.'

'What?'

'Dumbo did,' repeated John. 'He was an elephant and he flew. In the film. He had a magic feather and it ...'

'There's only one dumbo around here, and it isn't an elephant,' said Bright caustically. 'As I was explaining, if you put a bird and an elephant in a vacuum tube, the elephant would be able to fly just as well as the bird.' Bright gave a twisted grin. 'In other words, not at all.'

'What?' John stared at the tube. 'You'd never fit a bird and an elephant in there! And if you could, they wouldn't be able to breathe. It'd be cruel.'

Bright groaned. 'I only said "if". I wasn't proposing to do it!'

John followed Bright out of the lab and back up the stairs to the kitchen. 'I still don't see what all this has to do with Hardman.'

'This weightlifting contest is going to be a trial of brain versus brawn, right?' John nodded. 'Now, there's no way I can win a trial of strength with Hardman. I think we can agree on that?'

John eyed his friend's stick-insect body. Bright was surprisingly strong for his weight, but nobody would call him muscle-bound. 'Absolutely. But you're cleverer than he is,' John said loyally.

Bright snorted. 'So's a whelk. Logically, the only way I can win is if my weights are lighter than his.' John gawped at him. 'Look,' Bright went on, 'why does a fifty-kilogram weight weigh fifty kilograms?'

John's eyes narrowed. 'Is this one of those riddles like, Why did they bury Elvis Presley on the side of a hill?'

Bright looked puzzled. 'I don't think so. Why did they?'

'Why did they what?'

'Why did they bury Elvis Presley on the side of a hill?'

'Because he was dead.'

Bright, as usual, missed the point of the joke. 'It's not a riddle at all. A fifty-kilogram weight weighs fifty kilograms because that's the effect of earth's gravity on a fifty-kilogram mass.' He grabbed a felt-tipped pen and began to scribble mathematical equations on the message board stuck to the fridge door. 'A fifty-kilogram mass wouldn't weigh fifty kilograms on the moon, because the moon is smaller. It only has one-sixth the gravity earth has. So on the moon, a fifty-kilogram mass would only weigh fifty divided by six ... about eight kilograms. Actually, we shouldn't really talk about weight in kilograms, because, strictly, weight should be measured in newtons.'

John sighed. He'd thought he understood the names of weights. Evidently, he'd been wrong. 'I don't think,' he said slowly, 'you can arrange for the contest to take place with Hardman on the earth and you on the moon.'

'Don't be ridiculous!' Bright sighed. 'Perhaps I'd better try explaining this another way. Speaking of newtons, do you remember Isaac Newton and the apple? Newton was sitting under a tree, and an apple fell on his head. What do you think that told him?'

'That the tree he was sitting under was an apple tree?'

'No.'

'That the apple was ripe?'

'No.'

'That he was going to have a headache?'

'NO!' Bright ran a hand through his mass of spiky hair. 'He realized that there is some force coming from the earth that makes things fall towards it. Wait.'

Bright bounded upstairs. A few moments later he came back. He held up an object for John's inspection.

John scratched his head. 'Soap on a rope?'

'Exactly.' Bright held the end of the rope and started to whirl the soap around his head.

'Watch out,' said John. 'I think the soap's a bit soggy. It's starting to come off the rope.'

Bright ignored him. 'The soap is the moon,' he explained, 'and I'm the earth. The rope is the force of gravity.'

The soap flew off the end of the rope and shattered the kitchen window.

'And the window is ...?' prompted John helpfully.

Bright glared at him. 'The window is *B-R-O-K-E-N.*' He clicked his tongue in annoyance. 'However, it does illustrate the point. The moon is in orbit round the earth. Left to itself, it would just keep moving in a straight line for ever and fly off into space. But what Newton realized was that gravity pulls the moon towards the earth, and the earth towards the moon. So the moon is trying to fly away from the earth in a straight line, but gravity keeps it falling towards the earth at exactly the same rate, so it moves round the earth in a circle, more or less. Understand?'

'Of course,' said John crossly. 'It's not exactly rocket science, after all.'

'As a matter of fact, that's exactly what it is. Remember what I told you about the cow yesterday? Any spacecraft or satellite that's sent into orbit has to be moving in the right direction, at a speed that balances the force of gravity. If it's going too fast, it just shoots off into space. If it's too slow, it'll fall back.'

'All right, but what has all this got to do with Hardman and your stupid contest?'

'Oh, you'd be surprised.'

John felt himself go cold all over. There was a fanatical gleam in Bright's eye. John had seen that gleam before, and he knew that it meant two things. Bright had had an idea, and NO GOOD WOULD COME OF IT.

'What makes a fifty-kilogram weight weigh fifty kilograms is gravity,' said Bright. 'When we have the contest, Hardman's weights will be affected by the full force of earth's gravity. What I have to do to win is make sure that my weights aren't.'

John stared at him in disbelief. 'And how are you going to do that?'

Bright's grin was nuttier than a vegetarian cutlet.

'Don't worry,' he said softly. 'I'll think of something.'

CHAPTER FOUR

Hacking In, Stitching Up

'I've thought of something.' Bright's voice crackled tinnily over the telephone. 'Come round.'

It was Saturday morning. Typical! thought John. It never occurs to Bright that I might have something better to do with my time on a Saturday. Like … er … well, like watching rubbish on TV, or playing the video game I've already completed umpteen times, or going to the supermarket with Mum …

He went round to Bright's house.

'Good. You're here,' said Bright airily. 'I need you to help me get some equipment from my dad's lab.'

John scratched his head. 'But your lab is *already* full of your dad's equipment.'

Bright lowered his voice to a conspiratorial whisper. 'I'm talking,' he said, 'about the *other* lab.'

He led the way to an equipment rack on castors. With John's help, he shoved it to one side. Behind it stood a door.

John gazed at it with trepidation. The door into Bright's lab was made of steel and bristled with security devices, but it looked about as burglar-proof as a bead curtain compared to *this* door. *This* door looked as if it had been designed to protect the gold reserves of a particularly paranoid bank.

'Are you supposed to go in there?' asked John.

'Absolutely not!' replied Bright cheerfully. 'Dad lets me use the stuff in *here*.' He waved a hand at the equipment that almost filled his laboratory. 'He says I shouldn't be able to do much harm with it.'

John thought about the amount of harm that Bright *had* managed to do with the equipment in the lab, but said nothing.

'In *there*,' Bright continued airily, pointing at the newly revealed door, 'is all the stuff he thinks is too dangerous for me to use.'

John thought about equipment that even

Bright's dad considered too dangerous for Bright to use, and felt himself come over all faint.

'For a project like this,' Bright went on, 'I'll need some of the equipment from in there.'

'A project like what?'

'Now, I've already disabled the alarms. All I need to do is get the door open, and for that I need Dad's codes.'

'And how are you going to get those?'

'From Dad's computer.'

'Let me see if I'm following you here,' said John slowly. 'You're going to hack into your dad's top-secret files on his very own computer at MI5 ...'

'MI6.'

'... in the Ministry of Defence, and find the codes to get into this secret, hidden laboratory that he specifically told you never to go into. Is that right?'

'Correct.'

'Do you think that's a good idea?'

Bright snorted. 'Whether it is or not, if I'm going to beat Hardman at this challenge, I'm going to need some of the gear from in there. Time to go to work.'

He crossed the lab and sat at the computer. 'Oh, by the way,' he said carelessly, 'I finished that game you lent me. Thanks.' He dragged the game icon to the trash can. As the CD drawer slid open, he fished the disc out, returned it to its case and handed it to John.

'You finished it?' John stared at the game. 'Every level?'

'Every level.'

'How long did it take you?'

'A couple of hours.'

John sighed. It had taken him three weeks to get to Level 2.

'It was pretty simple,' Bright went on. 'I got a bit bored, actually, so I rewrote the game. You'll find it's much harder now.' He opened *Remote Access* and started tapping at the keyboard.

John, who had only been on Level 4 when he'd lent the game to Bright, groaned inwardly. He watched with a mixture of horror and admiration as Bright accessed the Ministry of Defence website and began to hack his way through the security levels.

At length, a message appeared on-screen.

Project Laputa.
Project leader – Prof. A. F. Bright.
Security clearance Alpha required to access this site.
MOST SECRET.

'Is that your dad?' John raised his eyebrows. 'A. F. Bright?'

Bright looked sheepish. 'Archimedes Faraday. Grandad was a bit of a science nut too.' He shrugged. 'In the department, they just call him

Archie.' He tapped his teeth with a biro. 'Why "Project Laputa", do you think?'

John thought hard. 'Laputa. I read about that once – I know! It's in *Gulliver's Travels*. Mum made me read it to Lulu. It's a flying island.'

Bright snorted. 'Flying islands! Hopelessly unscientific! Trust Dad to come up with a name like that. Still, this is what we want.' He tapped in another code. A message appeared on the screen.

Access Denied.
Do not try to open this file again.

There was a pause, and then another message scrolled across the screen:

This means you, Vernon.

Bright shook his head condescendingly. 'Oh, perlease!' He carried on tapping. Another message came up on the screen.

Vernon, can't you take a hint?

'Maybe you should stop there,' said John in a

rather squeaky voice. 'I think your dad really doesn't want you looking at this stuff.'

Bright frowned. 'He's just playing hard to get. This won't take long.' He tapped away for a while. Various messages appeared on the screen, each one increasing John's feeling of quiet panic.

I told you to keep out, Vernon. Go away.

You really don't want to do this, Vernon.

**If I find you've been into this file,
you are *sooo* grounded!**

Then the screen cleared. Lines of technical data and formulae appeared, all of it incomprehensible to John. Bright scrolled through it, muttering to himself and scribbling in a spiral-bound notebook.

Suddenly, there was a warning beep from the computer. The information on the screen dissolved into a random interference pattern. A dialogue box appeared and flashed a message:

**Unauthorized access detected.
Trace initiated.**

'They've spotted you! They're going to catch us!' John bit his lip.

Bright just looked annoyed. 'Calm down.' He tapped out a rapid series of commands. The computer began to emit a wailing noise, like a very unhappy siren. John stuffed his sleeve into his mouth and whimpered.

Another message box appeared:

Trace completed.

John gave a little moan of terror.

The message box disappeared and was replaced by another one:

Perpetrator of unauthorized access is:

<S White>7.Dwarfs@Fairyland.com/fooledya!

Bright hit the *Disconnect* command, looking smug. 'How good am I?'

John was shocked. 'You gave the computer a fake e-mail address? Isn't that illegal?'

'Of course I did. And yes, it is. Stop worrying. Everything's under control.' Bright tucked the notebook into his pocket. 'Come on. We're going to Dave's.'

'I thought you were going to get things from your dad's lab?'

'I can do that tomorrow. I need some stuff from Dave, and he's not open on Sundays.'

Bright and John found Dodgy Dave trying out a pair of powerful night-vision binoculars.

'New consignment, just in. Boy, oh boy,' he enthused, 'these babies are the business. Clear visibility over any distance, even on a night when you can't see your hand in front of your face.'

'And those are surplus to requirements, are they?' asked Bright innocently.

'They will be, one day.' Dave eyed Bright without enthusiasm. 'There is a school of thought,' he said loftily, 'that says that property is theft. I happen to be an honours graduate of that school.'

'A professor, I'd say,' corrected Bright.

Dave's eyes, behind their dark glasses, narrowed with suspicion. 'Lay off with the soft soap. What kinda darnfool stunt you tryin' ta pull now, Vernie?'

Bright frowned. 'Please don't call me that.' He

consulted his notebook, then held it out to Dave. 'Here's what I need.'

Dave read through the list. Then he gave a roar of laughter. '*Hasta la vista!* This time you gotta be kiddin', amigo! This is pure science fiction! What's this item here?'

John noticed that Dave's laughter sounded forced and his hands were trembling slightly as he held the notebook.

Bright gave him a hard stare. 'You know what it

is. You were trying to hide it last time we were round here. It's material from Area 51.'

Dave let out a small scream of horror. 'Holy cow! How did you know?' he gasped.

Bright shrugged. 'Just a guess.' His frown had turned into a hyena-like grin. 'Nice of you to confirm it.'

Dave slapped his forehead. 'I am such a satchel mouth! I just don't know when to zip it up.'

John was hopping up and down with excitement. 'Did you say Area 51?'

'Er, ahuh, ahuh.' Dave gave a not-very-subtle warning cough.

'Yes,' said Bright smugly. 'It's a –'

'Huge top-secret research base in America,' John interrupted. 'In fact, it's so secret that the American government says it doesn't exist. It was set up after a UFO was supposed to have crash-landed near Roswell.'

Bright gave John a quelling look. He wasn't used to his friend knowing more about any scientific subject than he did. Bright had forgotten that John was a science-fiction nut. 'Exactly,' he said in an aggrieved voice.

'Brilliant!' John's eyes gleamed as he turned to

Dave. 'People say that there are alien spaceships there and dead alien bodies and super-technological labs with all sorts of weird alien material inside.'

'That story's always been denied by the US military,' said Dave, playing for time.

Bright looked scornful. 'I'm sure it has.'

Dave made a final, desperate attempt to put Bright off. 'I can't let you have any of that stuff because there's no such thing!' he insisted, 'and even if there was, which there ain't, and even if I had any, which I don't, I still couldn't let you have it. Even the President of the Yoo-nited States isn't on the Need-to-know list for this material.'

'Where is it, Dave?'

Dave started to whine. 'Look, Vernie-baby, be reasonable. Cut me some slack here. What if the FBI found out it was missing?'

'The FBI *do* know it's missing. The MI6 computer files *say* they know it's missing. That's how *I* know it's missing. That's how I know *you've* got some.'

Dave hung his head in defeat. 'All right, already!' He pointed an accusing finger at Bright. 'Two conditions. One: I don't want to know what you need this stuff for, so don't tell me. Two: you didn't get this stuff from me, you don't know me, you never heard of me. Got it?'

'Don't worry.' Bright gave Dave a big, happy grin. 'You won't regret this.'

Dave gave him an unfriendly look. 'I'm regrettin' it already. When d'ya want this stuff?'

'I may as well take it now,' said Bright airily. 'John and I can carry it together if it's too heavy.'

Dave gave him a lopsided grin. 'Due to the nature of the material in question, this will not be a problem ...'

CHAPTER FIVE

Pigs Might Fly

John didn't get much of a chance to talk to Bright over the next few days. In school, Bright spent every lesson (no matter what the actual subject was) hidden behind a pile of books with titles like *Very Complicated Celestial Mechanics* and *New Developments in Quantum Physics*, scribbling notes. He spent all his free time in the library, growling at anyone who went near him.

This was frustrating, because John wanted Bright to show him what was in the boxes they had carried from Dave's yard to Bright's lab – boxes which weighed almost nothing, but were strangely hard to move or, once they were moving, to stop.

(John had got in between one of them and the gatepost of Bright's house and had almost been crushed.)

John finally decided to brave Bright's bad temper, and went round to his house. He found the back door unlatched. He stuck his head cautiously into the untidy Bright kitchen.

'Hello! Anyone at home?'

There was no reply. John looked around. The door to the cellar stood open. This was surprising in itself: Bright was very security-conscious. But when John, still calling 'Hello!', went through the door and down the steps into the cellar, he knew immediately that something was happening that was very strange indeed.

He knew this because as he stepped into the lab, Horace sailed past his head, bright button eyes alight with terror, and stumpy legs flailing away desperately in thin air.

'Prrrrrraaaaaaaaaarrrrrrrrrrrrr!'

John gawped. He wasn't astonished to find that Horace wasn't very good at flying. What was really astonishing was that he was flying at all: Horace was Bright's laboratory guinea pig.

'Prrrrrraaaaaaaaaarrrrrrrrrrrrr!'

John ducked as Horace made another pass, and stared past him. Bright was standing in the middle of the lab, holding something about the size and shape of a small cylinder-type vacuum cleaner. It had a strange-looking nozzle where the hose connection would normally be. Bright was keeping this nozzle pointed straight at Horace.

'What are you doing?' shrieked John in dismay.

'Oh, it's you.' If Bright was pleased to see John, he hid it well.

John pointed an accusing finger at Bright. 'You promised me you'd never do experiments on living things ever again!'

Bright kept the device he was holding focused on the guinea pig. 'I'm not experimenting on him,' he said indignantly. 'I'm giving him a stimulating new experience.'

'♪♪♪♪♪♪♪♪♪♪♪♪♪♪♪♪♪♪♪♪♪♪♪♪!' Horace did a barrel roll.

Bright began to sing.

He flies through the air with the greatest of ease,
This daring young pig doesn't need a trapeze ...'

'Stop it!' John reached out with both hands and caught the gibbering guinea pig as it flew past. He clutched Horace to his chest with one hand while the panic-stricken creature tried to climb inside his jacket.

Bright's machine was still pointing at Horace; now, of course, it was pointing at John as well.

Bright looked at John with his head on one side. 'Feeling a bit light-headed?' he enquired solicitously.

John's eyes widened. He did feel light. He looked down and gave a strangled cry. His feet were floating several centimetres above the floor. John began to flail about in alarm. Then he gave a shrill giggle. Having succeeded in getting inside his jacket, Horace was

clambering through a gap between the buttons of John's shirt. The combination of the guinea pig's sharp little claws and coarse fur was unbelievably tickly.

John flailed and writhed as he floated towards the ceiling. 'Stop – hee hee – it!' he shrieked. 'Hoo – turn – heee – it – hur hur hur – off!'

'Anything you say.' Bright flicked a switch. John's weight returned instantaneously. He tumbled to the floor in a heap and rolled around making gasping noises until he managed to drag the wildly struggling Horace out of his shirt. Then he sat up, looking very dishevelled, and glared at Bright.

'What is that thing?' he demanded.

Bright patted the machine proudly. 'My anti-gravity generator.'

'What does it do?'

Bright looked pained. 'I would have thought that was obvious. It cancels out the force of gravity.'

John was still feeling light-headed. 'Yes, I thought that's what it did.'

'How did you get in here, anyway?'

'You left the door open,' said John. 'The kitchen door, and the door into the lab.'

Bright looked concerned. 'I'm sure I didn't. I'm always very careful.'

'Well, they were open.' John stroked the

trembling guinea pig. 'Poor Horace. You've scared him half to death with your stupid machine.'

Bright was stung. 'It's not a stupid machine,' he said icily. 'It's an incredibly advanced piece of quantum-field engineering. What it does is very simple, but the way it does it is unbelievably clever.'

'The modesty transplant didn't take then?' said John sarcastically.

Bright wasn't listening. 'I told you once that light is carried in waves by particles called photons. Well, scientists have thought for some time that there are particles that carry the force of gravity. They're called gravitons, but they're very difficult to detect because, compared to electric and magnetic forces, gravity is very weak.'

'But you said that gravity keeps the moon in orbit round the earth ...'

'Yes, but the moon and the earth are very big. All objects give off gravitons, but unless the objects are absolutely huge, the forces can hardly be measured. You and I are both giving off gravitons at this moment, but you're not attracted to me, are you?'

'Absolutely not!' said John fervently. 'You're a friend, and that's it!'

'There you are then. I ...' Bright did a double take. 'I was talking about the attraction of gravity! Gravitons act on you, and me, and everything on this planet.'

'They weren't acting on Horace just now.' John put Horace back in his cage. The guinea pig burrowed deep into its sawdust bedding.

Bright gave the sort of self-satisfied look that made John want to heave a brick at him. 'No, and I'll tell you why. You've heard of antimatter, of course.' Without waiting for a reply, Bright went on, 'Normal matter is made up of atoms, and atoms are made up of particles. Some of these particles have an electrical charge. Protons have a positive charge. Electrons are negative.'

'I know how they feel.'

'But in antimatter, the charges are reversed. Antiprotons have a negative charge. Antielectrons, or positrons, have a positive charge. Now, imagine an antimatter universe.'

'I'm trying not to.'

'All the particles that we know about have antiparticles. So it makes sense that in an antimatter universe, there should be antigravitons.'

'I suppose so.'

'That's how my machine works. It produces antigravitons that cancel out normal gravitons. The result is that when I point the machine at something, the effect of earth's gravity on that thing is reduced. It becomes lighter.' Bright struck a dramatic pose and declared, 'No scientist in history has ever managed to detect gravitons, much less produce them. But I have! I have discovered a method to detect, and produce, not only gravitons but antigravitons!' He paused, impressively.

'Oh,' said John. 'Right. Good. Well done.'

Bright glared at him. 'Is that all you can say? This could be the greatest discovery since the wheel!'

'The greatest discovery since the wheel is how to make guinea pigs fly?'

Bright flew into a rage. 'You chuckle-headed, lame-brained numbskull! That was just a demonstration! The possibilities are almost endless ...' Bright broke off suddenly. He stared intently towards the door and held up a finger for silence.

'Did you hear that?'

John followed his gaze. 'Hear what?'

Bright took no notice. He was tiptoeing towards the door. Just before he reached it, and without warning, it slammed shut in his face.

John stared. 'Must be the wind.'

'That was no wind!' Bright wrenched the door open. There was a flicker of shadow at the top of the stairs as something – or someone, thought John – crossed between the door and the light from the kitchen window. But by the time Bright and John had clattered up the steps and checked the rest of the house and the street outside, there was no one to be seen.

Later that evening, Bright was still going on about how clever he'd been and how brilliant his invention was.

'Think what we could do with antigravity!' he burbled. 'Aeroplanes won't need wings any more! In fact, we won't need aeroplanes – people can just strap on antigravity belts and float wherever they want! You won't have to lug shopping home in carrier bags; you can have antigravity shopping trolleys. And suitcases. You could move whole buildings with the push of a finger.'

'There are houses on my street,' said John darkly, 'where you can do that already.'

'Yes, but they won't fall down, they'll just go wherever you push them. It could give a whole new meaning to "moving house". And what about space travel?'

John stifled a yawn. 'What about it?'

'Well, you'll be able to lift whole factories into space and keep them there for next to nothing. No more pollution!'

John yawned again.

Bright gave him a cunning look. 'It could even help you win your basketball match against the staff.'

John sat bolt upright. 'How?'

'Wait and see. I'll help you win the match if you help me win my bet with Hardman. Deal?'

John shrugged. 'I suppose so, but how?'

He was cut off by the insistent ringing of the doorbell. Bright looked startled. 'Who could that be?'

'Shall we sit here and guess?' asked John innocently, 'or do you think you should go and look?'

Tutting with annoyance, Bright went out into the hall. John heard the front door open. Moments later it closed again and a muffled figure sidled into the room.

John stared. The visitor was Dave, but he was wearing a trench coat with the collar turned up, and a wide-brimmed hat in place of his usual beret. What's more, he was behaving strangely. Strangely, John corrected himself, even for Dave. First, he flicked off the light switch, plunging the room into darkness.

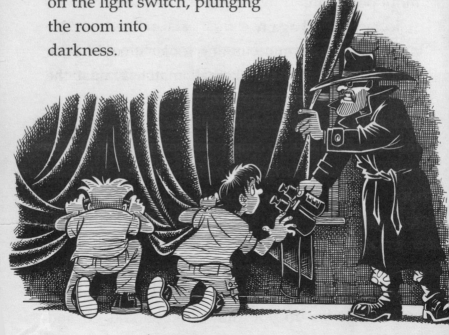

Then, keeping close to the walls, he crept around the room to the window. He slowly pushed the curtain aside to make a minuscule gap, pulled a pair of night-vision binoculars from his coat, and scanned the street. John and Bright watched, open-mouthed.

'C'mere.' Dave spoke out of the side of his mouth. Infected by his exaggerated display of caution, John and Bright crept to the window and made peepholes of their own.

'Take a look through these,' hissed Dave.

John took the binoculars and peered at the lamplit street. His eyes caught a movement in the shadows. His fingers gripped the binoculars more tightly. 'Oh!'

There was a man standing just beyond the light of the streetlamp. He could only be seen when he moved. As he brought the binoculars into focus, John could see that there was another man standing next to the hedge that belonged to the house opposite. There was a car parked further down the street with another man sitting in it. John saw him flick open a cellphone and start speaking into it.

'Let me see!' Bright snatched the binoculars.

John turned to Dave. 'Who are they?'

'I thought maybe you could tell me.' Dave let the curtain fall and slumped on to Bright's sofa. 'Two guys came to my place this afternoon. Real nosy types. They wanted to know, did I know you ...' he glared at Bright '... and where did I get my stuff from? Don't take no Einstein to figger someone's spilled the beans.'

'Well, it wasn't me!' protested Bright, still gazing through the binoculars.

Dave scowled. 'Chances are, you got careless hacking into your dad's files and they traced me through you.'

'Or that they traced *me* through *you* and your dodgy gear.'

'My gear is not dodgy!' Dave was affronted. 'I only deal in soon-to-be-obsolete, very nearly ex-military, almost-declassified, practically surplus materials. You know that.'

'Right. So you're under surveillance because ...?'

'We're all under surveillance,' Dave told Bright with a certain grim satisfaction. 'The guys out there are your very own spooks. Mine are still watching the depot. I gave them the slip.'

John wasn't convinced about the last statement.

Dave's idea of an 'inconspicuous' outfit made him stand out like a polar bear in the Sahara. He would have been less easy to spot if he'd been wearing a ballgown and riding a unicycle.

Bright was looking through the binoculars again. 'I wonder who they are?' he mused. 'My dad's people? MI5? FBI? CIA?'

'KGB?' suggested John.

Bright gave him a disgusted look. 'You watch too many James Bond films.'

'Hey!' John clicked his fingers. 'I bet it was one of them listening at the door this afternoon when you were telling me about the ...' he caught Bright's warning look and sideways glance at Dave '... the you-know-what,' he concluded lamely.

Bright nodded. 'That would explain how the doors came to be open.' He shrugged. 'Of course, they could just be people Dave owes money to.'

'OK, wise guy!' Dave dragged his hat down over his ears and turned his collar up still further. He stalked out of the room, turning at the door for a parting shot. 'Don't say I didn't warn ya! And remember – when those guys have got you strapped to a chair and they're makin' with the electric zapparoonies an' settin' fire to your socks

an' pullin' your toenails out with pliers –' he
paused and pointed a quivering finger at Bright,
'just don't come runnin' to me!'

CHAPTER SIX

Bright Throws His Weight About

'How do you spell "verruca", Watt?' demanded Ms Session.

'Er ... V-E-R-U-K-A?' hazarded John.

'How strange. That's exactly the way your mother spells it in this note you claim she wrote.'

'Well ... er ... she taught me to spell!'

'So, if I phoned her just now, she'd confirm that you are also suffering from ...' Ms Session paused and examined the note again, 'chilblains, tennis elbow, housemaid's knee and licky end.' She peered at John over the rim of her glasses. 'Which, as far as I know, is something you can only get if you're a pregnant sheep.'

John gulped and nodded. Had he overdone it? In any case, his form tutor could phone John's house until she was blue in the face. His mum was out at work.

Mr Hardman breezed in as the bell sounded for the PE lesson. He rubbed his hands together, giving Bright a crocodile grin. 'All ready then?'

'Apart from Watt,' Ms Session sniffed. 'He seems to have come down with everything from blackwater fever to hard pad.'

'Right, fine!' Mr Hardman barely glanced at John's clumsily forged note. 'If he wants to sit out, let him!' He strode off into the gym.

The rest of the class glared at John with a mixture of envy and incredulity. By all the laws of skiving, John had been caught bang to rights by Ms Session and should by now be standing in front of the bullet-scarred wall looking at the inside of a blindfold while the leader of the firing squad asked him if he had any last requests.

Today, however, Mr Hardman was clearly so preoccupied with the prospect of showing Bright up that he couldn't care less whether John was skiving or not.

John picked up his sports bag and gave his

classmates a shamefaced grin as they slouched off to the changing rooms, muttering darkly. Then he went into the gym and found a comfortable perch on a pile of unused mats.

Five minutes later, the rest of the boys in John's class shuffled into the gym wearing their PE kit, still casting discontented looks in his direction.

Terry McBride and Mick Philips sat Bright down on a bench and began massaging his calves and shoulders in a businesslike way. They seemed to be whispering advice and encouragement.

The rest of the class were looking sour-faced. Evidently they didn't think advice and encouragement were much use against an opponent with roughly four times Bright's body weight and the muscles of a gorilla with a private gym.

Mr Hardman clearly didn't think so either. He came in like a boxer on his way to the ring, bouncing on the balls of his feet. He was followed by Ms Session.

School gossip had it that Vivvy Session (John and Bright's form tutor and biology teacher) and Mr Hardman were 'an item'. There was much speculation on whether they would get married, and, if so, what their kids would be like. Terry

McBride was taking bets on it. The clever money was on 'something that has to be kept chained up in a cellar and fed through a tube'.

Ms Session was also one of the school first-aiders. She had a robust approach to injuries – kids had been known to walk home on broken legs rather than submit to her tender mercies. Today she was carrying a green box with a white cross on the side. 'I have a free lesson,' she explained, 'and Mr Hardman told me somebody might be needing my services shortly,' she went on, staring at Bright like a vampire eyeballing a particularly juicy neck. (Bright kept interrupting her in class. He kept correcting her. He did things to hamsters. Ms Session wanted to see Bright squashed like a bug.)

Mr Hardman cracked his knuckles. 'Right. Let's get started. I'll have the bar set at a hundred and fifty kilograms.'

While Simon West and Muzzie Rashid struggled to slide the weights on to the bar, Mr Hardman made his preparations: he pulled off his tracksuit top to reveal a singlet and a professional-looking weightlifter's belt. He wound bandages round the palms of his hands. Ms Session stepped forward, smirking, and shook powder over his hands. He prowled to and fro, with his eyes on the barbell, like a caged lion contemplating an unofficial breakfast of zookeeper.

Simon and Muzzie secured the weights on the bar and stepped back.

Mr Hardman approached the bar in the approved Olympic-Weightlifter manner. He grabbed the bar with both hands, twisting his grip like a motorcyclist revving up for a wheelie.

He swivelled his feet.

He dropped into a crouch and straightened his back.

He took four deep breaths, blowing his cheeks out like some exotic species of tropical fish.

'Ah – hoo, ah – hoo, ah – hoo, ah – *hoooo*.'

Eyes bulging, neck muscles tightening like ships' hawsers, Mr Hardman heaved at the weight, hauling it up to chest height. He paused for a moment.

'Ah – hoo, ah – hoo, ah – hoo, ah – *hoooo*.'

Veins bulged in his temples as he straightened his legs, wobbling slightly.

'Ah – hoo, ah – hoo, ah – hoo, ah – *hoooo*.'

Gritting his teeth, and with the groan of a man suffering from terminal constipation, Mr Hardman

raised the weight above his head. He held it there for a second or two, then let it crash down. With a self-satisfied leer on his livid, crimson face, he punched the air in triumph, then held his hands aloft to acknowledge the half-hearted applause from the class, and a series of jubilant American-chat-show whoops from Ms Session.

Then he turned to Bright and grinned like a ghoul.

'Your go,' he said.

'OK,' said Bright carelessly. 'But I'd like a bit more weight on the bar.'

Mr Hardman turned an unhealthy shade of purple. 'More weight?!' Then he shrugged and gave Bright a leer. 'Whatever you say ...'

'How much do you want on, Bright?' asked Simon.

'Three hundred kilograms.'

Mr Hardman's jaw dropped. He looked like a startled pelican. 'Don't be ridiculous! That's more than the world record,' he protested. 'For any lift. For any bodyweight.' He glared at Bright with a nasty glint in his beady little eyes. 'OK! Fine! Make a fool of yourself. Happy to oblige!'

As Simon and Muzzie struggled with the massive weights, John surreptitiously unzipped the top of his bag. Sliding one hand inside, he felt for the power

switch of the concealed antigravity machine and switched it on.

A low, muffled hum sounded from the bag. To John's relief, it was drowned by the chatter of the class.

Wringing his hand where he'd trapped a finger underneath one of the weights, Muzzie stepped back from the bar. A second later, Simon followed.

Bright glanced quickly at John.

Almost imperceptibly, John nodded.

Bright stepped up to the weight. He spat on his hands. He bent down, not bothering to keep his back straight.

He lifted the weight.

Just like that.

Bright lifted three hundred kilograms of dead metal as if it weighed no more than a stick of seaside rock.

John sat quietly behind the class and the teachers. Nobody noticed the concentration with which he was holding his sports bag so that one end of it pointed exactly at the huge weight. Bright began nonchalantly lifting the barbell from his knees to his shoulders – up and down, up and down – humming a little tune as he did so.

Mr Hardman's eyes swelled to the size of hard-boiled eggs. A muscle in his cheek twitched uncontrollably. He made a half-strangled moaning noise.

Ms Session dropped the first-aid kit and gave a small, breathless squeak, like a hedgehog on a busy dual carriageway realizing that it can forget its plans for the rest of the evening.

The rest of the class just stood gawping in wonder.

'And now,' said Bright casually, 'one-handed.'

True to his word, he took his left hand from the barbell and lifted the weight above his head with the right.

Then he held it out to the side and started twirling it as a drum majorette twirls a baton. Beads of perspiration appeared on John's forehead as he concentrated on keeping the antigravity beam from Bright's machine focused on the weights. Trust Bright to show off!

'Mmmuuurrrgggghhhh!' said Mr Hardman.

'Gggaaarrrooggghhh!' agreed Ms Session.

Terry McBride finally found his voice. 'Nice one, Bright!' He turned to the rest of the class. 'Here we go, here we go, here we go!'

The rest joined in. 'Here we *go*, here we *go*, here we *go*-ho!'

Bright, twirling the weights round his head, swapping them from hand to hand, occasionally flicking them so that the barbell leaped and spun through the air above his head, led the class on a lap of honour around the gym while Mr Hardman's legs buckled and Ms Session clung to the wallbars for support.

With a supercilious smile, Bright set the weights down again to rapturous applause. John switched the machine off. Bright turned to Mr Hardman.

'Over to you.'

Mr Hardman was speechless with rage. He pointed a trembling finger at Bright.

'Sabotage!' he hissed. 'You've jinxed the weights. I don't know how you did it, but you must have replaced them with plastic or something.'

'He didn't, sir.' Muzzie held up his damaged finger for inspection.

'Shut up, Mustaq!' Mr Hardman stood breathing deeply and glaring at Bright.

Bright looked pained. He indicated the weights. 'See for yourself,' he offered.

'Oh, I will!' Mr Hardman clenched his jaw until the bones creaked. 'I don't know how you did what you just did, but one thing I do know: I can lift anything you can lift. Nobody's going to make a monkey out of me!'

With those words he squatted down and hauled at the weights.

'Ah – hoo, ah – hoo, ah – hoo, ah – *hoooo*.'

Nothing happened.

'Ah – hoo, ah – hoo, ah – hoo, ah – *hoooo*.'

The weights completely failed to rise in any way.

'**Ah – hur, ah – hur,** *ah – HUUUURRRGGGH!*'

Mr Hardman suddenly stopped straining. His eyes took on a preoccupied look. He let go of the bar, but didn't get up.

'Viv!' he said in a hoarse whisper. 'I think I've done myself an injury, Viv.'

With a gasp of dismay, Ms Session rushed to him and started tapping his back.

'Does this hurt?'

'**AAARRRGGGHHH!**'

'Oh dear, Rodney, I think you've slipped a disc.'

'Oh, Viv.'

'Or it could be a hernia.'

'Oh, Viv!'

'Come on, we'd better get you to the medical room.'

Unable to straighten up, Mr Hardman took Ms Session's hand and shuffled out of the room in a pigeon-toed crouch, looking for all the world like a gigantic chimpanzee with its trainer.

As soon as they had gone, everyone in the class laughed themselves sick.

Bright's sudden popularity had gone to his head.

'I am brilliant!' he exulted as he and John walked home. 'I am so brilliant, somebody will have to

invent a new definition of the word "brilliant" just for me, that's how brilliant I am.'

John gave him an unfriendly look. 'Congratulations,' he said cuttingly. 'And you did it all by yourself too.'

'That's right.' Bright was impervious to sarcasm.

John seethed. 'Listen, Mr I'm-brilliant-and-don't-I-know-it, what about me?'

Bright gave him a look of genuine surprise. 'What about you?'

'*Who* had to keep those weights in the antigravity field while you were chucking them about like a mad juggler? *Me*, that's who! And it wasn't easy!'

Bright waved his hand dismissively. 'Well, I'm letting you carry the machine home as a treat, aren't I?'

'Oh, thank you very much ...' John broke off and stopped so suddenly that Bright cannoned into him.

'Ow!' Bright rubbed his nose, which had collided sharply with John's shoulder. '*Now* what's the matter?'

John was staring fixedly at the window of a house just ahead of them. He and Bright were reflected in it. Behind them, a sleek, black MPV, which had been cruising slowly along behind them, was just pulling into the kerb. Two men were sitting inside. They were wearing raincoats and, despite the dullness of the day, dark glasses.

John reached out and gripped Bright's arm. 'Don't look now, but I think we're being followed.'

Bright took a casual look over his shoulder. 'Oh, them! I know all about them. They followed us to school this morning.'

'You never told me!'

'It didn't seem important.' John stared at Bright. 'Look, this is Britain in the twenty-first century,' Bright continued calmly. 'They're just following us to try and find out what we're up to. I dare say they'll want to talk to us at some point. I doubt very much that they'll take us to the underground lair of some deranged psychopath with a white cat, who feeds people that annoy him to piranha fish.'

John still looked unhappy. 'Look, why don't we just give them your machine? Then they'll leave us alone.'

'In the first place, because I invented it and it's mine. In the second place, because I don't know who they are yet – my dad's people or someone else's. And in the third place, because we haven't finished with it yet. Don't you want to win your basketball match?'

John groaned. 'You keep saying your machine's going to help us win, but you've never explained *how*.'

'Later. Come on, and stop worrying.'

But Bright himself might have been worried had he known what was happening a few streets away, where Terry McBride and Mick Philips were waiting at a bus stop and talking about the events in the gym.

'Did you see Hardman's face?' Terry giggled. 'Wicked!'

'And the way Bright was chucking those huge weights about?' agreed Mick. 'Awesome, just awesome ...'

He broke off. A young woman in a dark suit and a young man in a dark raincoat seemed to have materialized just behind them.

'Excuse me,' the young man said quietly. 'Might we have a word with you at this time?'

Terry stared at them. 'Who are you?'

The young man took out a wallet. He flicked it

open to a section with a plastic window and displayed an identity card. The card had a photograph on it, and three very well-known initials.

Terry gulped.

'Oh, wow!' he breathed.

CHAPTER SEVEN

Basket-Work

Friday was the day of the staff-versus-boys basketball match. The last lesson of the day had been cancelled and the gym was full to the rafters with smug-looking staff, grim-faced boys and angry-looking girls. Even having a lesson cancelled wasn't enough to put a smile on the face of the students: the girls were furious at being left out and the boys knew they were going to witness another thrashing by the staff.

John stood in the middle of the basketball court, kitted out in team colours. It was the first time he'd ever been picked for any school sports team, but he wasn't feeling particularly cheered by the fact. He knew that Mr Hardman had chosen him because he was to basketball what Peter Rabbit was to sumo wrestling. Even Bright's team talk hadn't inspired him.

'Don't worry,' Bright had told the students as they changed into their kit. 'You're going to be the first team ever to beat the staff.'

This had been met with a disbelieving chorus of 'Oh yeah?'s, 'You reckon?'s and, 'Are you mental, or what?'s.

'Have belief in my ability,' Bright had replied.

'Don't you mean we should have belief in our own ability?' asked one of the players frostily.

'Oh, no.' Bright patted his sports bag in an enigmatic sort of way.

Only John knew what Bright intended, but even this knowledge couldn't remove the apprehension he felt.

As the start time approached, John glanced across at the staff team, who were limbering up purposefully. Mr Hardman, despite his recent injury, had insisted on playing. He was joined by Mr Allen (science and sarcasm), Mr Grimshaw (maths and moaning), Mr George (social science and shouting), Mr Peters (design technology and detentions), Mr

Jones (PE and picking on people) and Mr Robinson (computers and condescension). Most of them were lean and they all looked very mean.

In comparison, the students were a variety of shapes and sizes. Hardman had done a good job in selecting the worst team ever to represent the school. They consisted of Year Sevens, no-hopers and the two least-promising physical specimens Hardman could find: Bill 'Who Ate All The Pies' Balshaw would have been a perfect weight for his height if only he'd been a metre taller, and Pete 'The Bat' Potter was so-called because he was practically blind without his glasses.

Even then Hardman was taking no chances. He ran over to The Bat and snatched his spectacles from him. 'No glasses on court, Potter. What do you think we're playing, quidditch?'

Pete staggered away, arms outstretched, and promptly walked into the far wall.

And just to make sure that the students had *absolutely* no chance of winning, Mr Hardman had arranged for the Head and Deputy to referee. Ms Session was also in attendance with her 'magic sponge'. It was 'magic' in that people recovered dramatically from crippling injuries rather than have it used on them. Nobody knew what was on the sponge, though a mixture of aftershave, horse liniment and battery acid was most people's best guess. She was obviously praying that she would have to use it.

John decided to take responsibility for team morale. He called the players round him. After a slight delay while The Bat found his way to the middle of the court, the team went into a huddle.

'OK, look,' he said, in what he hoped was a go-getting, motivational sort of voice, 'don't worry. Bright's got something up his sleeve. I can't tell you what it is. Just don't panic if you start to feel a bit ... light-headed.' Looking round, John clenched his fists and finished his team talk with a rousing call to arms. 'Come on, we can do it, can't we!' he cried enthusiastically.

'Mumble, mumble,' came the reply.

'Say it! We can do it!'

'We can do it.'

'Say it louder!'

'We can do it, maybe ...'

John sighed and looked over at Bright. He really hoped that Bright's plan would work. Otherwise, they didn't have a hope.

Bright looked maddeningly unconcerned. He gave John a thumbs-up and made his way to the back row of raised seating. He sat down and placed his bag carefully on his knee.

Meena Patel was sitting next to Bright. She stared at the bulging bag. 'Have you got a wax blaster in there? Are you going to pump up the team and get them going, hey?'

Bright smiled mysteriously. 'It's not a music centre, but it will get them ... ah, up for the game.'

Before Meena could investigate further, there was a chorus of cheers and wolf whistles from the student crowd as Vicky Savage and a group of her mates from Year Nine ran on to the court. Vicky and the Savages, as they were known, were the cheerleaders for the school rugby team. They had been chosen for their ability to strike terror in the hearts of the opposition. Indeed, visiting teams had been known to run screaming from the rugby pitch following the Savages' pre-match dance ritual. Rumour had it that under their pompoms, the Savages wore knuckledusters and their trainers had steel toecaps.

Vicky lined up the Savages in front of the crowd.

They began their war dance with a blood-curdling chant.

'*Give us an S, give us a T, give us an O, give us another O, give us a D, give us an E, give us an N, give us a T, give us an S. What have we got ...?*'

Clearly, nobody had the heart (or the bottle) to tell Vicky that her spelling left a lot to be desired.

'*STOODENTS!*'

There was a half-hearted cheer from the students. Vicky stopped waving her pompoms and glared menacingly at the stands. The noise increased dramatically.

The Head shooed the glowering Vicky and her Amazons to the side of the court and called the teams together.

'Right, let's have a good clean game and may the best side win. And,' he added, not entirely in jest, 'if it isn't the staff, I'll sack them all! Let the game begin!'

PEEP!

The first few minutes of the game were not a pretty sight.

The staff barged, bumped and crashed their way into a quick twenty-point lead. Another thrashing was on the cards. The students in the crowd groaned.

Ms Session, on the other hand, was whooping and leading the staff celebrations. 'Hah! Eat that, suckers!' she screamed as Mr Hardman grabbed the ball out of John's hands and crashed into Pete Potter. The Bat didn't see what had hit him and lay on the ground, groaning.

'Go, Rodney!' Ms Savage shouted as Mr

Hardman pirouetted through the remainder of the school team, leaped skywards and slam-dunked the ball into the basket. He punched the air triumphantly. 'Watch and learn, boys! You're lucky you've got someone like me to teach you. Teachers like me don't grow on trees!'

No, they usually swing from them, thought John. He picked the ball up and looked towards Bright. Come on, he thought, it's time.

Bright obviously thought so too. He reached into the bag and flicked a switch.

Back down on the court, Mr Hardman ripped the ball from John's grasp. He threw it towards Mr Robinson (computers). As the ball flew over his head, John jumped in a feeble attempt to intercept the pass.

'Whaahh!' he cried out as he found himself shooting upwards. Even though he had been expecting it, the effect of the antigravity machine was startling. John recovered his wits and plucked the ball from out of the air. Landing, he sprang up and over the astonished Mr Hardman and bounded in great kangaroo-leaps towards the basket. The crowd were wide-eyed as John flew above Mr Jones (PE) and Mr Grimshaw (maths).

John hovered above the hoop and dropped the ball.

The students rose as one. 'Yeeeessssssssss!'

Meena Patel's jaw dropped. 'Nice hang time.'

Bright smiled to himself.

Even the girls forgot their grievances and began urging the student team to greater effort. Vicky and the Savages waved their pompoms with renewed enthusiasm.

'STOODENTS, STOODENTS!'

The pattern of play changed instantly. Suddenly, the students could run faster and jump higher than the staff. Four-foot-nothings seemed to float past staff defenders. The basketball seemed to have a mind of its own as it defied all the laws of gravity. Simple passes from the students suddenly became scoring shots as the ball flew towards the basket and dropped in.

Within minutes, the students had equalled the staff's score and then taken the lead with a Pete Potter shot that started as an unintentional backpass and changed direction several times before plopping through the hoop.

The students went crazy. For the first time in living memory, the school team were leading against the staff. Pompoms waved, kids chanted and Ms Session was forced into a sullen silence.

The staff team was being run ragged. The looks on their faces were ones of bewilderment and anger (mostly anger in Mr Hardman's case) as the students rattled up the points. As the fourth quarter began, the students were leading 34–22.

'Unbelievable,' muttered Meena. 'It's the stuff of dreams.'

'Not at all!' Bright was enjoying himself. He made a swooping movement with his bag and the ball, which had been about to drop into Mr Hardman's hands, shot past his ear for another basket. 'It's the stuff of science!'

'Ea-sy! Ea-sy!' chorused Vicky and her pompom-wielding banshees. The chant was taken up by the rest of the students.

John's confidence was soaring. They were going to win! He made another salmon-like leap over the staff defence. He was at the top point of the jump when his full weight returned in a split second. He fell to earth with a resounding thump and lay sprawled on the court while Mr Hardman, recovering from his surprise, scooped up the spilled ball and scored.

What had gone wrong? John turned to the stands in bewilderment. Bright wasn't looking at the court. He was staring fixedly at the door to the gym. John turned to follow his gaze.

The gym door was swinging back and forth. A tall, dark figure stood on each side of the doorway – a man and a woman, both dressed in black and wearing sunglasses.

Instantly, John guessed what had happened. The spooks had turned up at exactly the wrong moment. Obviously Bright had seen them and switched off the machine before they saw him using it. John turned back to Bright, who had slipped the bag under the bench and was sitting stock still, trying to look innocent. He gave John an apprehensive look and a helpless shrug. John's heart sank.

Without the machine, matters on the court changed immediately. John tried to intercept the ball and crashed into Mr Hardman. He fell to the ground, winded.

PEEP! 'Foul! Free shot,' judged the Head.

Mr Grimshaw (maths) gratefully accepted the opportunity. Over the next few minutes, the teachers once again began to score points at will. With just ten seconds to go, they had narrowed the student lead to a single point. 36–35!

The student crowd was hushed. The anxious spectators kept glancing at the clock and hoping that their team could hang on.

Mr Hardman had other ideas. He snatched the ball from Pete Potter and headed towards the basket. With just two seconds left, Mr Hardman lined up his shot. There was complete silence as the basketball left his hand.

The ball arced towards the hoop.

John could hear his heart thumping against his chest. The clock moved towards zero.

Bright's eyes flitted from the ball to the spooks and back again. He made his decision. Snatching up the bag, he leaped to his feet, aimed, and flicked the power switch.

A smile began to spread on Hardman's face.

The spooks' heads swivelled as their eyes locked on Bright.

The basketball hit the backboard and dropped, heading plumb for the centre of the basket rim. Hardman turned and began to pump the air in triumph.

His celebrations were premature.

Instead of dropping through the hoop, the basketball hovered at the rim for a second, then shot up, hit the ceiling and dropped on to Ms Session's head.

No score!

The buzzer for time sounded and the students went wild. Hardman's face was a mixture of astonishment, disbelief and fury.

While the other players on the student team mobbed each other, John turned an anxious face towards the doors. Bright's actions had been achieved at a cost. The spooks knew where the machine was. The man headed up the nearest aisle, towards Bright. The woman scanned the court – and headed straight for John.

Both had reckoned without the irresistible stampede of kids that suddenly descended on the court to congratulate their team. Urged on by the Savages, cheering spectators surged down from the seating. The unlucky agents were submerged beneath a tidal wave of ecstatic supporters and pompoms.

By the time they had pulled themselves together, sunglasses askew and dark clothes covered with footprints, the gym was empty. Bright and John were nowhere to be seen.

*

If only the spooks had hung around the gym for another half an hour, they would have seen Bright and John emerging from their hiding place under the seating.

'All clear,' said John. He shuffled his feet. 'Thanks.'

'For what?'

'For winning the game for us.'

'I'll probably live to regret it.' Bright gave John a wry look. 'You certainly made an impression on Vicky Savage.'

'How do you make that out?'

'Well, she gave you a great big hug, didn't she?'

John's eyes widened. 'Is that what she was doing? I thought she was mugging me. I gave her my pocket money.'

'Come on, let's get home.' Bright hauled the bag out from its hiding place. 'Before any more people in suits turn up.'

The two boys pelted across the gym, flung the door open and crashed into Mr Hardman. The bag thumped into his shins.

'Ow, Bright! You idiot!' Mr Hardman rubbed his bruises and eyed the bag. 'What are you two still doing here?' he demanded.

'Er – nothing, sir.'

A suspicious light flickered in the depths of Mr Hardman's little piggy eyes. He turned the full force of his gaze on Bright. 'Did you have anything to do with that …' he paused and gave a little twitch, 'basketball match?'

Bright was the picture of innocence. 'Me, sir? Oh no, sir, I wasn't playing, was I, sir? You didn't select me, sir.'

'Hurrrrr.' Mr Hardman gave the growl of a Rottweiler that has lost its bone and is getting ready to make whoever has it very, very sorry.

Bright gave a brittle smile. 'Well, must go, sir. Bad luck with the match. It seems that science beats muscle once again.'

John groaned. Bright could always be relied on to say the wrong thing.

Mr Hardman's cheek twitched. 'Really? And how was that, I wonder?' He looked down and his beady eyes narrowed into slits. 'What have you got in that bag?'

He snatched the bag from Bright, opened the zip and peered inside.

Bright gave a yelp of protest, but made no move.

Mr Hardman gave Bright a nasty smile. 'Taken

this from the science lab, have you?'

'No, it's mine,' protested Bright. 'Isn't it?' he continued, turning to John.

'Yes,' confirmed John.

'So you say.' Mr Hardman's smile racked up another five notches on the nastiness scale. 'I'll have to verify this with Mr Allen.'

Mr Hardman pulled the zipper shut with a flourish. Bright went rigid with shock. John gulped. As he closed the zip, Mr Hardman's thumb had flicked against the ON switch.

Bright heard the hum as the machine started up.

He stared in horror at the bag. 'I need that back, sir. It's mine. I need it now.'

Mr Hardman was too busy gloating to notice the humming sound from the bag. 'Need? Need! Amongst the many things you *need*, Bright, are some manners. The bag stays with me. It'll be safe in here.' He casually tossed the bag into the equipment store, slammed the door and locked it with the key he wore like a talisman on a ribbon round his bull neck.

'We'll see if that equipment is from the science lab on Monday morning,' he said. 'If it isn't, you can have it back then. But if it is ...' He left the threat hanging in the air.

'But, sir –' Bright cried desperately.

'I said Monday!'

Mr Hardman stormed out.

'Never mind,' John consoled Bright. 'He can't prove it's not yours, so you'll get it back on Monday.'

Bright turned to John and shook his head miserably. 'That's not the point! Didn't you see? He switched it on, the ignorant ape.' Bright bit his lip. 'Monday might be too late ...'

CHAPTER EIGHT

The Over-the-moon machine.

By Monday morning, Bright had chewed the nails off his fingers, the cuffs off his pullover and the straps off his schoolbag.

'There's no point in worrying,' John pointed out as they set off on their way to school.

'Ha!' Bright turned on him savagely. 'That's all *you* know!'

'What are you panicking about? We haven't seen the spooks since Friday.'

'Only because they don't know where my machine is and they're waiting for me to bring it out again. But that's not what worries me. I've never had the antigravity generator turned on for more than a few minutes, and now it's been left on all weekend. I've no idea what it might do.'

John began to get a familiar sinking feeling in the pit of his stomach. Not another Bright disaster! 'It'll just make whatever it's pointing at weigh less, won't it?' he said hopefully. 'And it'll stop doing even that when you switch it off.'

Bright avoided John's eyes. 'Probably.'

John's spirits went down like a lift in the *Titanic*. 'Probably?'

'Well, I had to work everything out in a hurry. I didn't get the chance to double-check all the equations.' Bright's face was paler than normal and his voice wasn't altogether steady. 'Some of them suggested that the effect might be ... cumulative.'

John's face fell. 'You mean, it might sort of build up, over time?'

Bright nodded glumly.

'But it'll stop when you turn the machine off, won't it?'

'Probably.'

'I wish you wouldn't say "probably" like that. I hate it when you say "probably".'

'Well, I don't know! It might be perfectly OK ...'

Bright tailed off. They had turned the corner and stood facing the school.

A breeze had sprung up, quite suddenly. It snatched litter from the gutters, wrapping it around the legs of pedestrians and plastering it against cars and fences. It whipped up dust and sent it, stinging, into faces.

Bright was staring fixedly at the school.

John followed his gaze. 'Oh dear,' he said.

Above the school, the sky was moving. A column of air was turning and shimmering, twisting like the dust cloud of a small tornado. As they watched, a stray sheet of newspaper detached itself from the branches of a tree and was swept into the whirling column, where it raced skywards. Moments later, a crow, cawing frantically and beating its wings for all it was worth, flew above their heads, going backwards. It was sucked into the mass of moving air and shot upwards like a jet fighter.

John turned an apprehensive face to Bright. 'What's happening?'

Bright looked as if his worst fears had been realized. 'I don't know for sure. But I don't like the look of it at all.'

'Oh, it's you two.' Mr Hardman treated John and Bright to the sort of look Vlad the Impaler must have given his enemies when he didn't have a spike handy.

'We've come to collect our bag,' said Bright in a subdued voice.

'Please, sir,' added John quickly, giving Bright a surreptitious kick on the shins, which he hardly appeared to notice.

'I dare say you have.' Mr Hardman puffed his chest out. 'Come down to the gym. I've asked Mr Allen and Ms Session to meet us there. You can explain to all of us *exactly* what you've got in there and what it does.'

Bright groaned.

Mr Allen and Ms Session were standing outside the gym when Mr Hardman arrived with Bright and John. Mr Allen looked wild-eyed and kept muttering to himself. Ms Session was leaning against the wall and breathing quickly. Mr Hardman stared at both of them in amazement. 'What's wrong?'

Mr Allen nodded towards the door of the gym. 'There's something very peculiar going on in that room.'

Mr Hardman gave him a bewildered look and reached for the door handle.

'No, Rodney!' Ms Session reached out and grabbed his wrist. 'Don't go in there!'

'What?'

'We went in there ...' Ms Session turned to Mr

Allen for confirmation, but he had started muttering again. 'I suddenly found ... I couldn't walk properly.'

Mr Hardman's face was a picture of blank incomprehension. 'What ... you fell over?'

'No! I mean, I couldn't keep my feet on the ground. I started to float away ...' Ms Session's voice rose to a hysterical pitch as Bright and John exchanged appalled glances. '... I had to climb down the wall bars.'

'You had to climb *down* the ...' Mr Hardman turned a furious face to Bright. 'What's happening?' Before Bright could reply, the PE teacher had squared his shoulders. 'Never mind. Whatever you've got in that bag, I'm going to take it out.' He reached for the door handle again.

'No, Rodney! It's too dangerous! Let someone else do it.'

Mr Hardman brushed aside Ms Session's restraining hand. 'I have to go, Viv,' he said quietly. 'This is my gym.'

He opened the door and went inside.

From the moment he entered the gym, as Bright and John could see through the glass panels of the doors, Mr Hardman was in trouble. Every step sent him bounding into the air, and he took longer to come down every time. His feet could find no purchase on the floor; eventually, they seemed hardly to touch the floor at all. He turned back towards the door, his face a study in fury, astonishment and frustration, and began to make swimming motions.

'He's coming back!' Ms Session's face was pressed hard against the glass. 'Oh, thank goodness!'

Threshing frantically at thin air, blue-faced and gasping, Mr Hardman finally reached the wall bars.

'He made it!' Ms Session clapped her hands in glee. Mr Allen, peering over her shoulder, grunted. John heaved a sigh of relief.

They had all underestimated Mr Hardman's resolve. He twisted round, braced himself against the wall bars – and flung himself in a flat dive towards the door to the equipment store on the opposite wall of the gym.

'Rooooooodneeeeeeeey!' Ms Session's despairing wail split the air.

Mr Hardman reached the door and grabbed the handle to steady himself. With his other hand, he fished out the key to the store on its piece of ribbon.

He turned the key in the lock.

He opened the door.

A hail of balls, bats, hoops, sticks and cones exploded out of the store. The PE teacher was engulfed in a cloud of sports equipment, which swept him up and away from the door. With a thunderous clatter, the contents of the store slammed into the roof – except where they slammed into the body of Mr Hardman, who was now spreadeagled on the gymnasium ceiling, staring in horror at the floor seven or eight metres below.

'Viiiiiiiiiiiiiiivvvvvvvvvvvvvvvv!'

Bright gave a low moan. Through the open door of the equipment store (which was flapping around as it tried to tear itself off its hinges) he could see John's kit bag sitting squarely in the middle of the floor. A faint green glow surrounded it.

'Rodney! Come down!' screeched Ms Session. She turned frantic eyes on Bright. 'What's happened to him?'

'Bright!' bellowed Mr Allen, making a grab for him. 'You've got some explaining to do!'

But Bright wriggled away from the science teacher's clutching fingers. He and John hared away down the corridor, with the screams of Mr Hardman, the shrieks of Ms Session and the furious roars of Mr Allen echoing in their ears.

Bright and John crouched behind the groundsman's shed on the school playing fields, watching bits and pieces of debris shoot past to feed the growing vortex that hung above the gym. From behind them came the sounds of a school in uproar.

John's teeth were chattering. 'What h-h-happened?' he stuttered.

Bright was clearly rattled. 'What I was afraid would happen! The zero-gravity field has grown stronger and expanded. And it'll go on expanding! As long as the machine is switched on, it'll keep growing bigger and bigger and bigg –'

John grabbed the front of Bright's pullover and shook him. 'Then we've got to turn the machine off!'

'And how are we going to do that?' Bright wailed. 'We can't get anywhere near it! If we go too close, we'll just join Hardman on the ceiling! Or if we're not so lucky, we'll smash straight through the roof, shoot miles up into the air, and then fall thousands of metres and get spread all over the landscape.' Bright mimed the fate in store for them. 'Wheeee – splat – dead!'

'And that's what'll happen to Hardman if the gym roof doesn't hold and he flies through it?'

'Yes. If he doesn't just fly off into space and die horribly from explosive decompression.'

'Oo-er.' John decided he probably didn't want to know what explosive decompression was. He risked a peek round the corner of the shed.

The twister hovering over the school was visibly growing by the minute. Exercise books flew in circles, shedding pages. Curtains flapped around like demented ghosts. Pans from the school kitchens danced crazily in an upward spiral. The school had been evacuated, and the buildings were surrounded by bewildered pupils and shell-shocked staff, who were moving back slowly as the edge of the antigravity effect advanced inexorably towards them.

'What's happening?' wailed John.

Bright took a deep breath. 'The machine's created an antigravity field around itself. That field is growing. Everything around the machine is becoming weightless, so it's falling away from the earth. Remember, the only thing that holds anything down to the earth is gravity. The machine's taking the gravity away.'

'So everything around the machine is going to fly off into space?'

'I'm afraid so.'

'Including the school?'

'Eventually, yes.'

'So, it isn't all bad?'

'But it won't be just the school.' Bright ducked as a flight of roofing tiles shot past, whirring like a flock of pigeons, and disappeared into the antigravity vortex. 'See? It's reached the houses round the school already! It'll pick up anything that isn't stuck down – cars, boats, caravans ...' Bright gave a gulp. 'People.'

John was thunderstruck. 'People!'

'All animal life! Horses ... dogs ...'

John stared across the field to where a little black Scots terrier had wandered to the furthest extent of its retractable lead and had been picked up by the antigravity field. The little dog was now howling in panic as it flew on the end of its lead,

like a small hairy kite, with its frantic owner trying desperately to reel it in.

'... cows,' moaned Bright.

John whistled. 'If a cow got sucked into the antigravity field, it really *could* jump over the moon.'

Bright held his head in his hands. 'Then it'll start on everything that *is* stuck down,' he went on. 'Houses, shops, offices ... but that's only the start of it.' Bright gave a hollow groan. 'Think of a fountain in a garden pond. A pump forces the water up into the air, and it falls back into a reservoir, and just keeps going round and round. But what would happen if the water didn't fall back?'

'Well, you'd run out of water because ...' John tailed off. 'Oh,' he said in a small voice. 'So this is quite bad then.'

'Exactly. Right now, up there ...' Bright jabbed a finger skywards, '... air is being pumped out into space. At the moment, most of it is probably falling back down because as it drifts sideways, away from the area affected by the machine, the earth's gravity grabs hold of it again. But if the machine's effect keeps growing, earth's atmosphere will gradually be pumped away into space. Eventually, all the air on the planet will be lost for ever.'

'In fact,' John went on in awed tones, 'it could be the end of the world as we know it.'

Bright shook his head. 'No it won't.'

'Oh!' John gave a sigh of relief.

'It'll be much worse than that.'

'Oh.' John sank back into the depths of despair.

'Eventually, the whole planet will weigh nothing. It'll break out of its orbit around the sun and fly off into interstellar space. The molten core will expand. Any water that remains will boil off into space. The whole planet will disintegrate into a cloud of dust. It won't just be the end of the world as we know it,' said Bright in a hollow voice, 'it'll be the end of the world, full stop.'

John gave a low moan. 'I'll say one thing for you. When you foul up, you *really* foul up.' He looked around apprehensively as the shed began to shake.

'The antigravity field's reached us,' said Bright tightly. 'Come on!'

They turned away from the school and ran. Behind them, the shed tore itself apart. Its roof, flapping like a giant bird, flew into the vortex, followed by the walls. The school mower was snatched up and sucked into the storm too. Lightning flashed inside the spinning cloud of debris.

John and Bright reached the fence and climbed into the road, which was a mass of jostling cars, each with a sofa or sideboard tied to its roof by frantic householders trying to get out of the path of the antigravity tornado with whatever belongings they could salvage. It was like a scene from a war zone.

People scurried about, some pushing bikes with TV sets precariously balanced on the handlebars, others carrying birdcages or fishbowls. One woman was trying to cart her fridge away in a pushchair. The two boys stared about them in horror.

'You've really done it this time, Vernon.'

Bright and John spun round. Standing behind them, flanked by a young man in a dark overcoat and a young woman in a dark suit, was a figure in a white lab coat. His arms were folded across his chest. His piercing eyes glinted at them over half-moon glasses. He was the picture of righteous indignation, from the toes of his scuffed shoes to the topmost tuft of his spiky, unruly hair.

Bright stared up at him. His shoulders slumped.

'Hello, Dad,' he muttered.

CHAPTER NINE

Dave's Finest Hour

'And exactly what did you use for the casing?'

'Well, er …'

'Don't rush,' said Bright Senior grimly. 'We have all the time in the world.'

The interrogation was taking place in a large truck, parked several streets away from the antigravity zone. From the outside, it looked like a removal van, but the inside was packed full of all kinds of electronic equipment. Professor Bright was using it as a mobile command centre.

John sat in a corner being ignored; which was, he thought resignedly, something he was good at. Worried-looking people in white coats scurried about, and security agents in dark suits kept coming and going, along with uniformed police and army officers. Bright's father ignored them. He stood with his arms folded, glaring at his son.

Bright twisted uncomfortably in his seat. 'Look, I don't want to get anyone into trouble ...'

'Depends what you mean by "trouble".'

Professor Bright's voice dripped sarcasm. 'If you define trouble as "being flung thousands of miles into space away from the smoking remains of the earth", I'd say you'd already got all of us into that kind of trouble. Did you have some worse kind of trouble in mind?'

Bright threw his hands in the air. 'All right, all right. I used some of the stuff from Area 51 …'

Bright Senior tore out a few handfuls of hair. 'Area 51?! How in the name of Isaac Newton did you get hold of material from Area 51? … Wait a minute!' Bright's father clicked his fingers. 'You used that for the casing?'

'Yes, I did.'

'Brilliant! That alien metal lets gravitons pass straight through it, so it weighs almost nothing –'

'– and blocks antigravitons, so that anything inside it is shielded from the antigravity effects it produces. I know,' said Bright complacently.

Bright Senior pounced. 'How do you know?'

'Uh …'

'Because you looked into my computer files, didn't you, Snow White? If we survive this, I'm going to kill you.'

'But what I don't understand,' wailed Bright, 'is

why my machine is doing all this ...' He waved his hand to indicate the chaos that reigned outside. 'It's only supposed to produce a stream of antigravitons to affect things it's pointed at. That's how I designed it!'

'And it might even have worked like that if it had been properly constructed! If I know you, you probably threw it together as fast as you could, with no thought of proper shielding or fail-safes – so now, it's pumping out antigravitons in all directions.'

'Like radiation from a leaky microwave oven!' offered John.

'Exactly!' Professor Bright stared at John for a moment, clearly trying to remember who he was. He gave up and turned back to Bright. 'You didn't answer my question. Where did you get the stuff from Area 51?' Bright's father bent down until he was eyeball to eyeball with his son. 'And don't even *think* about not answering.'

With a sigh, Bright gave him Dodgy Dave's name and address. Bright's father snapped his fingers. A couple of heavy-looking men in dark suits came over. Following a whispered conference, they left in a hurry.

Bright Senior turned back to Bright. 'Now, while we're waiting for your friend to show up, we'd better start trying to find a way out of this mess.'

For nearly an hour, Bright and his father hammered at computer keyboards and scribbled furiously on notelets, which they stuck up all over one end of the van.

Professor Bright's team rushed about like so many white-coated ants, carrying computer print-outs, fetching materials, tapping at calculators, arguing. Everyone completely ignored John, who spent the time peering glumly at a monitor screen showing pictures from the van's roof-mounted camera. On the screen, the ever-expanding twister rose, roaring, into the sky above Bright's anti-gravity machine. The van was forced to pull back twice as the antigravity field expanded.

At length, Professor Bright's heavies returned with the remainder of the Area 51 material from Dave's warehouse. They also brought in Dave himself, looking very subdued.

The professor called him over straight away. 'Mr Vickers, some of my colleagues will probably want to have a word with you about your suppliers later on.' Dave nodded miserably. 'Right now, any practical help you can give my team on working with the alien metal would be of value.' He tapped a screwdriver handle on one of the equipment racks. Silence fell.

Bright Senior scanned the anxious gathering. 'All right,' he said, 'we have two plans to deal with the current – ah – situation. Plan A: we build a suit out of the alien metal and send someone into the affected area to switch the machine off. Since the suit will block antigravitons, the person who wears it will retain their normal weight and should be able to move around quite freely.' He looked around. 'No guarantees though – we haven't got time to produce a proper armoured suit, so we'll have to bodge together something crude but – hopefully – effective. It may work, it may not. So, while the suit's being built, Vernon and I will be working on Plan B.'

Several members of the team fixed Bright with hostile stares.

'Vernon and I have talked about the methods he used to build his – ah – device,' Professor Bright went on, 'and I'm going to attempt to produce a force field that will reverse the polarity of the particles being generated by his machine. This means that the machine will start producing gravitons, rather than antigravitons, and the weightless effect will gradually be cancelled out.'

'Professor!' One of the white-coated boffins waved urgently. 'Isn't there a danger that such a field would reverse the polarity of other subatomic particles and perhaps produce a region composed of antimatter?'

John remembered Bright saying that antimatter was the reverse of normal matter, but that was all he could remember without his brain wobbling.

Bright's father gave a nervous grimace. 'We think that's unlikely.' He spread his hands. 'In any case, unless anyone has a more workable suggestion, I really don't see that we have a great deal to lose.' There was a tense silence. 'OK, people,' Bright Senior concluded briskly, 'let's make it happen.'

The meeting broke up. Engineers and scientists scurried to their allotted tasks. Dave turned to Bright's father and saluted. 'Permission to speak, sir?'

Professor Bright gave him an exasperated

glance. 'I'm not a soldier, Mr Vickers, and neither are you. What is it?'

'I just wanted to say, sir, when the suit is finished, I'd like to volunteer to put it on an' go switch that blamed machine off. I kinda feel it's my dooty.'

'We have specially trained operatives, who are better equipped to handle this kind of situation.' Bright Senior smiled wanly. 'Personal feelings don't come into this.'

Dave nodded resignedly.

One of the white-coated engineers beckoned him over. 'I'm Dr Myers,' he said. 'Professor Bright has briefed me to lead Team A. We have to produce a suit out of the stuff from your depot, but my engineers seem to be having some trouble drilling it.'

'You need a slow drill speed,' said Dave immediately. 'Try to drill fast, and that stuff just hardens up on you, but it'll cut like aluminum if you take it easy.'

'That's the sort of know-how we need. Come over here, will you?'

Now deep in conversation with Dr Myers, Dave went to join the team assembling the suit.

John waved to attract Professor Bright's attention. 'Professor! What can *I* do?'

Bright's father shot him a dismissive glance. 'Stay out of the way.'

Feeling hurt and left out, John retreated to a relatively uncrowded corner of the van. On the way, he caught the sleeve of the man who had asked the question during Professor Bright's briefing. 'What if this force field *does* make everything inside it into antimatter?' he asked.

The man gave him a worried look. 'If that happens, as soon as the force field is switched off ...' He threw his hands wide. 'Blooowie!'

'Blooowie?'

'The antimatter, and an equal amount of normal matter, will totally annihilate each other in a vast explosion that will blow the earth to smithereens and possibly take out half the solar system.'

John blinked. 'That's not good.'

'Of course, it may not happen.' The man bustled away.

John glanced around the van. Bright, his father and several more people with white coats and anxious expressions were busy assembling another machine.

John sidled across to where Bright was working. 'What's going on?' he hissed from the corner of his mouth.

Bright didn't look up. 'When this device is ready,' he said in a tense mutter, 'it will create a kind of force-bubble with the help of repeater stations that other teams will set up all around the antigravity zone. The repeater stations are simple focusing devices – this is where the field will be generated. Hold that wire, will you? ... No, there ...' He soldered the connection and reached for another component.

'So it's not going to blow up the world then?'

'I shouldn't think so. Probably not.'

'You know I told you how much I hate it when you say "probably"?' Bright nodded. 'Well, I hate it even worse when you say, "probably not".'

John crossed his fingers behind his back.

Several more hours of feverish activity passed. The antigravity vortex continued to grow relentlessly.

'That's it.' Dr Myers finished riveting a seam on the helmet and held it out to a special services agent, who was already encased in the alien metal.

ked like the Tin Man from *The Wizard of Oz*.
o try Plan A.'

Dr Myers checked the fastening of a rope that
was tied to a handle on the front of the suit. 'This
is your tether. If you feel yourself floating away, fix
it to something solid.'

He draped coils of rope over the agent's
armoured shoulder, then indicated the camera that
had hastily been fixed to the top of the helmet.
'Check your video and voice links when you get
outside. Good luck.'

With a curt nod, the agent took the helmet and
climbed ponderously out of the van. His team
immediately turned to the monitor screen at the
front end of the van, waiting for the video picture
to come through.

Nobody saw Dodgy Dave pick up a spare
wrench, and slip out the back door of the van.

Bright made another connection. 'Almost there.'

'I thought I told you to keep out the way.'
Professor Bright stood behind John, glaring.

'He's been helping me.'

John held up a circuit board as an alibi.

'Oh, all right. Just don't waste time. According
to the computer models, if we're not ready in

twenty minutes, we won't have enough power to contain the antigravity effect.'

'We'll be ready,' Bright assured him.

'We'd better be.' Bright Senior spun to face the video screen. 'What's the hold-up over there?'

Dr Myers looked worried. 'I don't know, sir. We should have the video link by now.'

'Try the voice link.'

'Yes, professor.' Myers flicked a switch. A voice came from the speaker below the screen.

The voice said, 'Aaaaaaahhhh!'

Myers picked up a fist mike. 'Douglas. Agent Douglas. Do you copy?'

The voice from the speaker said, 'Uuuuurrr.'

'Agent Douglas. This is Command One. Do you copy?'

A faint voice from the speaker said, 'Stand by, Command One.'

The video screen flickered and cleared to show a picture of the street outside the van. There was an outbreak of cheering and high fives from the Plan A team. The picture began to move.

'OK, Douglas. We have you on sound and vision. The boundary of the antigravity zone is fifty metres dead ahead.'

'Copy that, Command One.'

Dr Myers gave a nervous start. Professor Bright raised his eyebrows. 'Something wrong?'

'Well, professor, I know it's crazy, but … that doesn't sound like Douglas's voice.'

Bright Senior's eyes widened. At the same moment, there was a confused hammering from the back of the van, and the door was flung open. Agent Douglas half-fell into the van. His armour was missing. He was rubbing the back of his head.

Professor Bright snatched the mike from the stunned Dr Myers. 'Mr Vickers, come back here!'

'Sorry, colonel!' Dave's voice, coming from the speakers, sounded positively cheerful. 'Like I said – this is my party.'

Bright's father gestured frantically at the remaining spooks. 'Stop him!'

'Too late.' Dr Myers's eyes were glued to the picture on the monitor screen, which showed objects whipping past from behind the camera and flying up into the antigravity vortex. 'He's crossed the border.'

CHAPTER TEN

What Goes Up ...

Every eye in the command-centre vehicle was focused on the monitor screen.

John whistled softly as he gazed at what was left of Elmley School.

The temporary classrooms had long gone. As John watched, the roof was hauled off the school hall and torn to shreds by the swirling vortex above. The prefabricated parts of the school buildings were disintegrating before his eyes. The roof tiles on the older buildings were missing. Only the brick walls and a few of the better-constructed buildings had survived. One of these was the gym.

Dave's progress was painfully slow. The wind

snatched and whipped at his armoured body as he crawled through the ruined buildings.

'Whoa! Ain't seen a mess like this since Typhoon Mary wrecked my apartment,' said Dave.

John turned to Bright. 'That must have been some storm.'

Bright, who was guiding Dave through the ruins, shook his head. 'She was an old girlfriend of Dave's.'

John blinked. 'Dave had a girlfriend? What was she like?'

Bright gave John a sickly grin. 'Don't ask.' He spoke into the fist mike. 'Left into the corridor, Dave. About twenty metres, and the gym's on the right.'

'Copy that.' Dave's breathing was ragged with the effort of pulling himself onwards. A swirling dust cloud blanked the screen for a while, then Dave's voice came over the speaker. 'OK, I'm there.'

John leaned forward. 'It's going to work! He's going to make it!'

As the picture cleared, the anxious watchers could see the doorway of the equipment store in the opposite wall, a few metres away – and inside the doorway, the squat, menacing shape of Bright's antigravity machine. The green glow now filled the whole store and spilled out into the gym.

'OK, Dave.' Bright's voice was hoarse. 'You can see the machine. All you have to do is flick the switch on the top to ...'

'Heeeeeeelllllllllllppp!'

The voice could hardly be heard above the roar of the wind.

Dave's head jerked up. 'What in tarnation?'

The camera now showed a picture of the gymnasium roof. Mr Hardman's mottled face and bulging eyes were clearly visible on the screen.

John gave a gasp of horror. 'Hardman! I'd forgotten all about him!'

Dave's voice crackled from the speaker. 'Who is that guy?'

'Our PE teacher.' Bright turned an appalled gaze to John. 'We can't just leave him up there ...'

'Heeeeeeelllllllllllppp!'

Professor Bright snatched the microphone from his son's hand. 'Now listen to me, Vickers,' he snapped. 'If you're having any thoughts about daring rescue attempts, forget them. Switch the machine off and he'll be OK. If you don't ...'

There was an ominous creaking sound from the speaker. On the screen, cracks appeared in the ceiling of the gym.

'I don't think that roof'll hold out till I reach the switch,' came Dave's voice. The camera angle changed to show the rope that Dave had shrugged off his shoulder and was now running through his hands.

'The switch!' Professor Bright's voice was a scream.

'No time!' Dave let go of the free end of his tether, which raced upwards like the world's fastest Indian rope trick. Several coils slapped on to the ceiling, and across Mr Hardman's face and upper body. The PE teacher frantically grabbed at the rope. At the same moment, with an ear-splitting roar, the gym roof was torn off.

Mr Hardman shot to the end of the rope and juddered to a halt, howling with fright. The picture jerked as Dave's feet were yanked off the floor. The watchers in the command centre held their breath.

Dave's agonized voice grated from the speaker. 'I'm being pulled up, off the floor … must … hang … on … Sorry, guys, I can't reach the switch.'

'Untie the rope.' Professor Bright's voice was deathly calm. 'Let him go.'

'No … way … José …'

The professor dashed the mike to the floor. 'That's it. We've no alternative. Activate Plan B.'

As Professor Bright barked orders, John grabbed Bright by the arm. 'He meant it, didn't he? Your dad? He really wanted Dave to let Hardman go.'

Bright looked wretched. 'It makes sense. One life for millions …'

John turned away.

'Vernon!' Bright Senior's voice sliced through the babble of scientists calling instructions to each other. 'Here! Now!'

Speakers linked to the command centre's radio sets crackled as the repeating stations reported in.

'*Station Five, ready.*'

'*Station Six, ready.*'

Bright Senior gazed fixedly at the clock set into the equipment array above the force-field generator. 'If we're going to do this at all,' he said tightly, 'we've got less than two minutes to do it.'

'*Station Ten, ready.*'

'That's all of them.' Bright looked up at his father.

'Throw the switch.'

Bright's finger jabbed down on the power switch of the force-field generator.

Nothing happened.

He tried again.

Still nothing.

'Er ...' said John.

Bright turned a frantic face to his father. 'It doesn't work!'

The professor was wild-eyed. 'It's got to! Didn't you check the dipolar conduits?'

'Er ... excuse me ...'

'Of course I did! Did you align the plasma field coils properly?'

'Ah ... could I just ...?'

'Do you take me for a fool? Did you calibrate the residual flux matrix –?'

'EXCUSE ME!!!'

Bright and his father turned to John in shock.

'I'm no expert,' said John, 'but wouldn't that machine work better if you plugged it in?'

Bright and his father gaped at John ... then at each other ... then at the power lead dangling uselessly from the side of the force field generator ...

Gibbering with panic, Bright grabbed it and

fumbled it into an unoccupied socket. He reached over and stabbed at the switch for a third time.

There was a deep electric hum. Tell-tale lights flashed on all over the machine. Dials lit up. Screens flickered. Bright stared at the read-outs.

'I think it's working,' he croaked.

Professor Bright led the stampede out of the van.

All around the border of the antigravity zone, the air shimmered. The creeping edge of the effect seemed to hesitate – then to hold still – then, very slowly, to retreat …

There were outbursts of ragged cheering. People shook hands, slapped one another on the back, hugged one another, sobbed with relief.

Then somebody looked up.

Next moment there were screams of renewed panic as everyone suddenly realized what was about to happen to all the hundreds of tons of material that had been sucked into the antigravity vortex and were now, once more, becoming subject to the laws of gravity …

John and Bright lay under the command-control truck and watched as a silver-grey Toyota crashed through a roof a few houses down the street.

Bright winced. 'Oh dear.'

John turned to look at him. Then he gave an insane giggle. Then he started to laugh, and laugh, and laugh.

'What's the matter with you?' demanded Bright indignantly. 'This is serious.'

'Oh, cheer up!' John cackled hysterically. 'After all, it isn't the end of the world ...'

Some time later, Bright and John helped to haul Dave out of the remains of the gym. His armour was so bashed and dented by the debris from the vortex that had fallen on top of him that he looked as if he had been chewed.

'Hoooowie, fellas,' he gasped as they finally succeeded in yanking the battered helmet from his head. 'I thought I was a goner for a while there. Then the good news – I was back on the floor. Then the bad news – that dude on the roof was coming down straight on top of me. Then the worse news – so was everything else.'

Bright cleared his throat. 'Er ... where is Mr Hardman now?'

Dave gestured at the pile. 'Under there. I managed to roll him underneath me so my armour would shield him some, but I reckon he still got hit pretty hard. If you listen real good, you can hear him hollerin'.'

John cocked an ear and listened. He turned a shocked face to Bright. 'I didn't think teachers were supposed to use words like that.'

Dave, who was in high spirits after his exploits, winked at Bright and John. 'I'd let someone else dig him out if I wuz you. I reckon you critters just dropped right off his Christmas card list, you know what I mean?'

'Secure the area!' Professor Bright was giving instructions to his team as John and Bright trudged back with Dave. He beckoned Bright over. 'As soon as the site is secure, Dr Myers is going to send a team in to dig that machine out and turn the blasted thing off. When that's done, we can switch off the force field. At some point after that, young man, you and I will be having a serious talk.' He turned on his heel and strode away.

Bright scurried after him. 'But, Dad! Aren't you going to stay to supervise the clean-up operation?'

Bright Senior gave him a hard stare. 'Look around you. How long do you think the clean-up operation is going to take?' He checked his watch. 'In any case, I don't have the time. I'm supposed to be finding a way to stop a giant comet crashing into the earth …' Professor Bright's mouth snapped shut. He gave Bright and John a guilty look. 'Ah, you should probably forget I said that.' He strode away and stepped into the back of a black limousine, which began picking its way through piles of debris.

Bright and John looked around. In front of them was a circular area, several hundred metres across, where hardly a house or tree was left standing. It looked like the result of a bomb blast. At its

centre, Elmley School had almost completely disappeared. Some distance away, a team of rescuers was leading a very dishevelled and dusty-looking Mr Hardman to safety.

John cleared his throat. 'It's going to take more than stopping your pocket money to pay for this lot.' He stopped, realizing that Bright wasn't listening to him. 'What's up?'

Bright was staring at the work party that had been sent to dig up the machine. They were clearly in some sort of trouble. The ones furthest from Bright's machine were stumbling away as fast as they could, while the ones nearer to it were crawling on hands and knees.

'What's the matter with them?' John turned a puzzled face to Bright. 'They look like you did when you were magnetic and you tried to get down ... those ... iron ... steps ...' He tailed off.

Dave, freed from his armour, appeared at Bright's shoulder. 'Say, dudes, do you feel ... like, heavier than usual, all of a sudden?'

Bright slapped his forehead. 'Oh, no!'

John's puzzlement had turned to horror. 'What? What?'

Before Bright could reply, there was a howl of

rage from behind them. Bright spun round and gave a yelp of terror.

A vengeful mob was heading towards the spot where he was standing. Leading the charge were Mr Hardman, Mr Allen and Ms Session. They were close to the remains of the school, and moving as if they were wading through treacle, but they looked determined. A few paces behind, the Head was dragging himself forward with a wild look on his face and what looked like a piano leg in his hand.

'My school!' he screamed. 'What have you done with my school?'

Behind the Head streamed the rest of the school staff and assorted householders, shop assistants, park keepers, motorists and other people obviously intent on causing Bright harm ...

'Don't you see what's happening?' Bright ran frantic fingers through his spiky, unkempt hair. 'Our plan has worked too well! The force field is too efficient. Right now, my machine is pumping out gravitons just as fast as it was pumping out antigravitons before, so everything – and everyone – around it is getting heavier. And you know what'll happen eventually!'

Dave and John stared at Bright in consternation.

'We'll get sucked right through the centre of the earth and end up in Australia?' suggested John.

'Worse than that.' Bright shook his head hopelessly. 'If it isn't stopped, the field will expand again, but this time the gravity field will increase until the earth collapses in on itself and shrinks to the size of a tennis ball.'

Dave shook his head. 'Wow, dude – this is heavy.'

The mob was now coming out of the increased gravity zone and starting to roll forward with increasing speed. Soon it was moving at full charge. Bright gave it one more appalled glance, and ran. He raced down the street with the mob at his heels, in the wake of Professor Bright's retreating car.

'Dad!' Bright's voice carried faintly on the wind to where John and Dave were standing, still rooted to the spot in shock. Bright leaped over piles of debris, like a scruffy, shock-headed gazelle, chasing the speeding limousine as if his life depended on it – which it probably did.

'Dad! Come back, Dad! There's a problem …!'